Wish for Love

OTHER BOOKS BY BARBARA CARTLAND

Historical:

BETWITCHING WOMEN
THE OUTRAGEOUS QUEEN (the story of Queen Christina of Sweden)
THE SCANDALOUS LIFE OF KING CAROL
THE PRIVATE LIFE OF ELIZABETH, EMPRESS OF AUSTRIA
JOSEPHINE EMPRESS OF FRANCE
DIANE DE POITIERS
METTERNICH—THE PASSIONATE DIPLOMAT
THE PRIVATE LIFE OF CHARLES II

Sociology:

YOU IN THE HOME
THE FASCINATING FORTIES
MARIAGE FOR MODERNS
BE VIVID, BE VITAL
LOVE, LIFE AND SEX
VITAMINS FOR VITALITY
HUSBANDS AND WIVES
MEN ARE WONDERFUL
ETIQUETTE
THE MANY FACETS OF LOVE
SEX AND THE TEENAGER
THE BOOK OF CHARM
LIVING TOGETHER
THE YOUTH SECRET
THE MAGIC OF HONEY
BOOK OF BEAUTY AND HEALTH
ETIQUETTE FOR LOVE AND ROMANCE
KEEP YOUNG AND BEAUTIFUL By Barbara Cartland
and Elinor Glyn
BARBARA CARTLAND'S BOOK OF HEALTH

Cookery:

BARBARA CARTLAND'S HEALTH FOOD COOKERY BOOK
FOOD FOR LOVE
MAGIC OF HONEY COOKBOOK
RECIPES FOR LOVERS
THE ROMANCE OF FOOD

Editor of:

THE COMMON PROBLEMS BY RONALD CARTLAND (with a
preface by the Rt. Hon. The Earl of Selborne, P.C.)
BARBARA CARTLAND'S LIBRARY OF LOVE
BARBARA CARTLAND'S LIBRARY OF ANCIENT WISDOM
"WRITTEN WITH LOVE" Passionate love letters selected by
Barbara Cartland

Drama:

BLOOD MONEY
FRENCH DRESSING

Philosophy:

TOUCH THE STARS

Radio Operetta:

THE ROSE AND THE VIOLET (Music by Mark Lubbock)
performed in 1942

Radio Plays:

THE CAGED BIRD: AN EPISODE IN THE LIFE OF ELIZABETH
EMPRESS OF AUSTRIA. Performed in 1957

General:

BARBARA CARTLAND'S BOOK OF USELESS INFORMATION,
With a Foreword by The Earl Mountbatten of Burma.
(In aid of the United World Colleges)
LOVE AND LOVERS (Picture Book)
THE LIGHT OF LOVE (Prayer Book)
BARBARA CARTLAND'S SCRAPBOOK
(In aid of the Royal Photographic Museum)
ROMANTIC ROYAL MARRIAGES
BARBARA CARTLAND'S BOOK OF CELEBRITIES
GETTING OLDER, GROWING YOUNGER

Verse:

LINES ON LIFE AND LOVE

Music:

AN ALBUM OF LOVE SONGS sung with the Royal
Philharmonic Orchestra

Film:

A HAZARD OF HEARTS
THE LADY AND THE HIGHWAYMAN
A GHOST IN MONTE CARLO
A DUEL OF HEARTS

Cartoons:

BARBARA CARTLAND ROMANCES (Book of Cartoons) has recently
been published in the U.S.A. and Great Britain and in other parts of the world.

Children:

PRINCESS TO THE RESCUE (A children's pop-up book)

BARBARA CARTLAND

Wish for Love

ROBERT HALE · LONDON

© Barbara Cartland 1983
This edition 1994

ISBN 0-7090-5084-4

Robert Hale Limited
Clerkenwell House
Clerkenwell Green
London EC1R 0HT

Printed in Great Britain by
St Edmundsbury Press Limited, Bury St Edmunds, Suffolk
Bound by WBC Limited

ABOUT THE AUTHOR

Barbara Cartland, the world's most famous romantic novelist, who is also an historian, playwright, lecturer, political speaker and television personality, has now written over 560 books and sold over 520 million copies throughout the world.

She has also had many historical works published and has written four autobiographies as well as the biographies of her mother and that of her brother, Ronald Cartland, who was the first Member of Parliament to be killed in the last war. This book has a preface by Sir Winston Churchill and has been republished with an introduction by Sir Arthur Bryant.

She has broken the world record for the last thirteen years by writing an average of twenty-three books a year. In the Guinness Book of Records she is listed as the world's top-selling author.

As a Dame of Grace of the Order of St. John of Jerusalem and Deputy President of the St. John's Ambulance Brigade, she has fought for better conditions and salaries for midwives and nurses.

She has championed the cause for the elderly, had the law altered regarding gypsies and founded the first Romany Gypsy camp in the world.

In 1984 she received, at Kennedy airport, America's Bishop Wright Air Industry Award for her contribution to the development of aviation when, in 1931, she and two R.A.F. officers thought of, and carried, the first aeroplane-towed glider air-mail.

In January 1988 she received 'La Médaille de Vermeil de la Ville de Paris' – the highest award given by the city of Paris for achievement – for 25 million books sold in France, and in March 1988 was asked by the Indian government to open one of the largest health resorts in the world.

In the 1991 New Year's Honours List Barbara Cartland was invested by Her Majesty the Queen as Dame of the Order of the British Empire for her contribution to literature and her work for humanitarian and charitable causes.

Author's Note

Highwaymen and footpads were regular dangers to travellers in the 17th and 18th Centuries. Most noblemen had outriders in attendance and if a Highwayman was caught he was hung on a gibbet at the crossroads, if he was shot it was considered a brave act deserving congratulations.

Many Highwaymen had been footmen or servants in great houses where they learnt to covet the luxuries of their Masters. They were well aware of the risks they ran but thought a few years of riotous living were preferable to a lifetime of drudgery.

Sometimes gentlemen took to the road. William Parsons was a baronet's son educated at Eton and had been an officer in the Royal Navy. Sir Simon Clarke was a baronet.

The only known woman Highwayman was Joan Bracey, daughter of a rich Northamptonshire farmer. Dressed in men's clothes she pulled off many daring robberies, but swung from the gallows before her thirtieth birthday.

CHAPTER ONE

1818.

Jeremy Forde walked into the Dining-Room, and as he did so he shouted:

'I am down!'

He then seated himself at the table in the window which was covered with a white cloth and at which the family usually had their breakfast.

In response to his shout his sister Mariota came from the kitchen carrying a plate of eggs and bacon in one hand, and a pot of coffee in the other.

'You are late!' she said.

'I know,' Jeremy replied, 'but I lay in bed thinking there was nothing to get up for and wondering how we could make some money.'

Mariota laughed.

'That is not in any way an original thought.'

'I know,' Jeremy said gloomily as he started to eat the eggs and bacon.

Mariota sat down at the table and having poured out a cup of coffee for her brother did the same for herself.

'I was thinking,' Jeremy went on, 'that if I sold one of the miniatures, which I believe would fetch a fairly good price, nobody would know.'

Mariota gave a cry of horror.

'But we should all know!' she protested. 'And you know as well as I do that not only would Papa be furious, but you would also be stealing.'

'There is nothing wrong with stealing from one's-self,' Jeremy argued sulkily.

'It would not only be from you,' Mariota said, 'but from

11

your son, your grandson and all the generations that come after them.'

'As things are, it is very unlikely that I shall be able to afford a son,' Jeremy retorted, 'let alone a grandson.'

He finished his eggs and bacon and sat back in his chair.

'Seriously, Mariota, we have to do something. I need some new clothes, not because mine are old, but because I have grown out of them.'

Mariota knew this was the truth and made a helpless little gesture with her hands.

'I am sorry, Jeremy, you know I am. But we hardly can afford to eat, let alone buy anything to wear.'

'Is there nothing Papa can do about it?' Jeremy enquired.

'You think of something,' Mariota replied, 'and I will talk to him about it, if he will listen to me.'

'Even if he does, I doubt if he will understand the straits we are in,' Jeremy said angrily.

There was a little pause. Then his sister said:

'I do not think that is true. Papa does understand, and because it hurts him to see the house going to rack and ruin and to listen to us complaining he tries to live in a world of his own with his books. It is the only way he can forget Mama.'

Mariota's face softened as she spoke of her mother, and Jeremy was silent until he said:

'We have to do something. How much longer can we go on like this?'

Mariota asked herself the same question not only every-day and every night, but almost every hour.

The Fordes had lived at Queen's Ford, their beautiful, rambling and very large but inconvenient house, since it had been built in the reign of Queen Elizabeth. But each generation had grown successively poorer and poorer.

When their father, Lord Fordcombe, had inherited the title and the estate they found that his father had run up a mountain of debts during the last years of his life.

Everything that was saleable and was not entailed onto the next heir, had been sold, and even then the creditors had been forced to accept ten shillings in the pound, thinking that half a loaf was better than no bread at all.

The new Lord Fordcombe had been left with the income from the capital his wife had brought with her marriage settlement and which was settled on his children when he died.

This brought in little more than £200 year, and his only other source of income was the meagre rents from his farms and some better class houses on his estate.

The cottages of which there were quite a number, were either occupied by pensioners or were in such a dilapidated state that only those who were otherwise destitute were willing to live in them.

The lack of money affected his three children to the point of desperation.

Jeremy was now twenty-one, but he could not afford to enter a Regiment as his forebears had done, and he resented violently having to live at home with only old hobbledehoy horses to ride, and nothing to do from morning until night except catch fish from the river and shoot in the woods.

This was a regular contribution to their needs, yet was no longer an enjoyable sport but a monotonous necessity.

For Mariota it was different because, since they could only afford to keep one old couple to run the house, the rooms would have been inches thick in dust if she had not constituted herself Housekeeper, house-maid, butler, footman, valet to her father and brother, besides being at times a cook when anything special was required.

Because she was practical and organised herself in what had to be done in such an efficient way, the family forgot that at nearly nineteen she would, if their circumstances had been different, have been having a Season in London, dancing at Balls, and receiving proposals of marriage from eligible bachelors.

There was no likelihood of anything ever happening while, as Jeremy said gloomily, they were buried in the country and looked more like turnips than ordinary people.

The only member of the family who had less reason for

grievance than her brother or elder sister was Lynne.

Not yet seventeen, she was fortunate enough to be exactly the same age as one of their neighbour's daughters, and it was therefore arranged she should share her lessons with her.

Every day she was collected by a carriage from The Grange, and if it rained or they particularly wanted her to stay the night, she did so.

Besides her other worries, Mariota worried about what would happen next year when Lynne was too old for lessons. She was lovely, so lovely that her sister could not help thinking that any young man who saw her would instantly go down on his knees and ask for her hand in marriage.

But there were very few young men in their part of Worcestershire, and as Squire Fellows, whose daughter she had lessons with, was very strict about young girls being kept in the School-Room until they were grown up, Lynne had so far not tasted the social life which Mariota longed for her to have.

If Lynne was lovely with her fair hair, blue eyes and pink-and-white complexion that made her look like a piece of Dresden china, Mariota was lovely too, but in a very different way.

Her mother had once said:

'Lynne is like a beautiful portrait by one of the great artists, with colours so vivid that it is difficult to think that anything could be more attractive. But you, my darling, are like one of the exquisite drawings by Leonardo Da Vinci, for once somebody has looked at you, they want to go on looking because there is so much to find beneath the surface.'

Mariota had not exactly understood this at the time, but sometimes she looked at herself in the mirror and remembered what her mother had said.

She thought with her large grey eyes and her hair that was so fair it seemed sometimes to be silver, she did in fact resemble some of the drawings she had seen in the books in the Library.

But she seldom had time to think about herself. When

14

she got up in the morning she twisted her long hair into a bun at the back of her head and hurried downstairs to start pulling back the curtains and opening the windows.

Being practical she had realised that it would be impossible to keep the whole house open without proper staff.

She had therefore closed off the wings on each side of the centre block which together formed the 'E' shape in which the house had been built as a tribute to Queen Elizabeth.

But sometimes she would go into the low-ceilinged and beautiful rooms with their diamond-paned windows and look at the dust on the floor and at the pictures and the furniture shrouded by covers, and feel that it was like the Palace of the Sleeping Beauty which would never again wake to life.

Then because it made her so depressed she would go away, back to the shabby, threadbare centre of the house which still rang with the sound of voices, footsteps and laughter, except when Jeremy was in one of his bad moods.

She knew now that one of his bad moods was coming on, and she said:

'Do not despair, dearest. I feel in some strange way that something is going to happen.'

'What do you mean?' Jeremy asked. 'That another ceiling will fall down or a chimney-pot drop off?'

'No, I do not mean that at all,' Mariota said seriously. 'Sometimes I have an instinctive feeling — what our old Nanny would call being "fey" and I am sure something exciting is coming towards us.'

'You have got bats in your belfry!' Jeremy said rudely. 'The only thing that is likely to come towards us here is a thunder-storm which will take more tiles off the roof, or a bill for something which has been forgotten and requires immediate payment.'

'Now you are being definitely unkind and horrid,' Mariota protested. 'Grumbling has never got anybody anywhere but dreams do sometimes come true.'

'Not as far as I am concerned!'

Then as he saw the hurt in his sister's eyes he smiled and

it made him look very handsome and attractive.

'Forgive me,' he said. 'I am behaving like a spoilt child and I am well aware of it. But you understand how frustrating it is.'

'Of course I understand,' Mariota replied, 'and it is worse for you than for any of us because you are the oldest.'

She paused before she said:

'And you are so handsome! Of course you want smart clothes and horses like those Grandpapa rode . . until he died and we found he had not paid for them!'

'At least he had some fun even if it was on credit.'

Jeremy drank his coffee, then looked round the Dining-Room.

'There is certainly nothing we can sell here,' he said, looking at the pictures of his Forde ancestors.

'There is nothing you can sell anywhere,' Mariota said firmly. 'We have been through all this before, Jeremy, and you know as well as I do that anything worth 6d. was sold when Papa inherited.'

'It is a pity he cannot sell his title,' Jeremy said, 'or his book which he has been writing for the last three years.'

Mariota gave a little sigh.

'When it is finished no one will want to buy it, as it is only about us and there are so few Fordes left.'

'And the few there are, are as poor as we are,' Jeremy finished.

He got up from the breakfast-table and as he did so he looked at the highly polished table which could seat thirty and which ran down the centre of the room. Then beyond it to where on a side-board Mariota had left a silver candelabra whose candles were lit every evening for dinner.

It was too much trouble to put it away every night in the safe, and Jeremy stared at it reflectively.

As if she knew what he was thinking Mariota gave a little cry.

'No, no, you cannot sell that, Jerry! It is in all the Inventories, and you know perfectly well that it was given to our great-grandfather by George I, and is an heirloom.'

Jimmy did not reply, then suddenly he said:

16

'I have an idea! If you will not let me steal from myself and the hypothetical sons I am very unlikely to have, I will steal from somebody else.'

'What do you mean? How can you be a thief?' Mariota asked.

'I am not going to be a thief, I am going to be a Highwayman!'

'You are crazy!'

'No, I am not. Do you remember when there was all that talk of a Highwayman in the vicinity two years ago who held up quite a lot of carriages and never got caught?'

'But, Jeremy, how could you do such a thing?'

'Why not? I am sure I am very much poorer and more in need of money than any Highwayman who ever terrorised travellers.'

'You are not . . serious?'

'Yes, I am!' Jeremy said. 'And now I think of it, you will have to help me.'

'Help . . you?'

'If Highwaymen have any sense they hunt in pairs. Otherwise, while one of them is taking money and jewels from the passengers in a carriage, the men on the box could shoot him in the back, or at least hit him with something.'

Mariota began to clear the breakfast things on to a tray.

'I am not going to listen to you,' she said. 'You are talking nonsense, and if you want something to do you might see if there are enough new potatoes in the garden for luncheon.'

Jeremy did not answer, but walked across the room to stare out of the window. Mariota looked at him apprehensively, thinking once again how handsome he was and how difficult it must be for him to have nothing to do but ride inferior horses round the estate which was as neglected and impoverished as the family who owned it.

She knew by the way he was concentrating and the expression on his face that he had one of his mad-cap ideas which she dreaded, because they invariably proved disastrous and landed him in a lot of trouble.

'You are not listening to me, Jeremy.'

17

'I have got it!' Jeremy ejaculated. 'We will go to the Worcester Road this afternoon. There are certain to be carriages containing rich people going either to Worcester or Malvern and we will pick out one and see if we can fill our pockets as Highwaymen have done for the last five hundred years.'

'How can you think of doing anything so ridiculous and so dangerous?' Mariota questioned. 'You must . . surely be . . joking!'

'I am not joking,' Jeremy said. 'I am going to have some money so that I can go to London just for a week and buy myself some decent clothes, and perhaps find an heiress whom I can marry.'

'An heiress?' Mariota exclaimed.

'Why not? If I can marry somebody rich and restore the house we could all live here in comfort. I want to be doing all the things I ought to be doing at my age instead of mouldering away like a rotten apple.'

The bitterness in Jeremy's voice was very apparent, and Mariota walked round the table to put her hand on his arm.

'I am sorry, dearest,' she said, 'but we will just have to go on hoping that something will turn up.'

'For how long?' Jeremy asked sharply. 'Until I am in the grave?'

Mariota had no real answer to this. She merely sighed and looked up at him and her grey eyes were very soft and sympathetic.

'No!' Jeremy said so loudly that she jumped, 'God helps those who help themselves! That is what I am going to do, and you are going to help me.'

'That is something I will not do!' Mariota said positively.

'Very well,' Jeremy said, 'I shall be a Highwayman on my own, and if I am shot in the back with a blunderbuss and lying in my own blood you will be sorry!'

'How can you say such . . wicked things?' Mariota asked.

'I am only being practical,' Jeremy replied. 'If you come with me there will be no danger. We will hold up a coach together. You can keep the coachman and the footman with their hands above their heads while I snatch everything

I can from inside. Then we gallop away and are never seen again!'

'I am sure it will not be as simple as that,' Mariota said feebly, 'and anyway, we might be . . recognised! Think of the . . scandal that would . . cause!'

'We shall not be recognised,' Jeremy said scornfully, 'because we shall be wearing masks. But wait — I have another idea! You will be dressed as a boy.'

'As . . a boy?' Mariota said faintly.

'All those old clothes of mine are hanging up somewhere. You will find a pair of breeches to fit you, and I am sure the riding-coat I wore when I was at Eton is about your size.'

'I cannot do it . . I cannot!'

'Very well, if you will not help me I will do it alone,' Jeremy said. 'Goodbye, Mariota! You will not have to put flowers on my grave because they will hang me from the gibbet at the cross-roads, as a warning to other Highwaymen.'

Mariota gave a cry of sheer horror.

'You cannot be serious . . you cannot!' she said pleadingly.

Even as she spoke she knew that in his usual impulsive manner Jeremy would become a Highwayman with or without her help.

. . . .

Riding from the house at four o'clock that afternoon Mariota was extremely conscious of how unladylike she appeared.

She was wearing a pair of breeches which Jeremy had worn when he was thirteen and a coat which was actually a little large for her. But there was nothing smaller in the wardrobe where all his old clothes had been put away when he had no further use for them.

She also wore a velvet hunting-cap pulled low over her forehead, and a well-tied cravat around her neck added to her disguise.

When they were some way away from the house in the

shelter of a small wood Jeremy pulled a black mask from his pocket and held it out to her.

'You must put this on,' he said. 'I made them this morning, and I am quite certain that once you wear it nobody will recognise you.'

Jeremy certainly looked unrecognisable behind his mask. Yet Mariota thought that with his tall hat on the side of his head, his broad shoulders and the way he sat his horse, it would be easy, even with the mask, for anybody if not to recognise him, certainly to remember him.

But she knew there was no point in saying so. They had argued most of the morning while Jeremy went on looking through his clothes for her to wear, and she knew that anything she said now was just a waste of breath.

When Jeremy made up his mind, she thought, it would take an earthquake to move him, and only because she was desperately afraid he was right when he had said that doing this crazy thing alone was dangerous had she finally consented to go with him.

Now she put on the mask, tied the narrow ribbon at the back of her head and hoped that in whatever lay ahead, her hat would stay firmly in place, otherwise her hair might come tumbling down and reveal that she was not the young man she pretended to be.

'Now take your pistol,' Jeremy was saying, pulling it from the pocket of his coat. 'It is primed and loaded, so be careful!'

'I do not have to . . use it . . do I?' Mariota asked in a low voice.

'Not unless it is to save yourself from being captured, in which case you will be hanged,' Jeremy replied. 'But if you do need to use it, shoot at the arm or the leg, not the body or the head.'

Mariota's lips tightened, but she did not say anything.

She was actually a good shot because when they were much younger her father had taught Jeremy to shoot first at a target before he attempted to shoot at live game, and she had pleaded to learn too.

'You are a girl. You will never have to use a pistol!' Jeremy had said scornfully.

Their father had contradicted him by saying:

'It is always useful for a woman to know how to defend herself.'

He had therefore taught Mariota to handle not only a shot-gun, but also a duelling-pistol, and although she hoped now she would never have to use it, she felt that she was experienced enough not to kill a man by mistake.

'Are you ready?' Jeremy asked. 'At least, Mariota, you must admit this is more exciting than sitting in the house and counting the cobwebs!'

Mariota did not reply because her heart was beating frantically and her lips felt dry.

She was quite certain that Jeremy's new idea would be disastrous, and already she was thinking how terrifying it would be if they were captured and taken before the Magistrates.

However, there was nothing she could say and she could only pray that her father would never know what they were doing.

He had luncheon with them, but he was in one of his most absent-minded moods, and she knew he was concentrating on some particular research he was doing into the family history.

Because Jeremy too had been concentrating on a very different project, the meal was almost a silent one, and as there was not much to eat, it did not take them long.

Only Jeremy exclaimed as Mariota brought in a dish from the kitchen:

'Not rabbit again!'

'I am sorry, dearest,' Mariota replied, 'but there is really so very little else at this time of the year, and it is the only thing we do not have to pay for.'

Old Jacob, who ran the house with his wife, caught them in snares in the shrubberies, and because there were plenty of rabbits and very little else, it had become their staple, if very monotonous diet.

There were however ripe gooseberries to follow, and the

bushes, which were vastly overgrown, had scratched Mariota abominably when she picked the fruit from them.

But while her father ate them like an automaton without appearing to taste what went into his mouth, Jeremy gobbled them up and said when he had finished the dish:

'I am still hungry!'

'I am afraid there is only a very little cheese left,' Mariota said, 'but Mrs. Robinson has promised me some this evening.'

It was Mariota who had arranged that the Home Farm, which had once been run to serve the big house, should be let to tenant farmers for an infinitesimal rent, so long as they provided them with eggs, milk, butter and when it was available, cheese.

At first the Robinsons had been very pleased with the arrangement, but now with the end of the war and the difficulties of peace, many farmers had become bankrupt and the rest were afraid of the future.

Because of this Mariota felt that the farmer and his wife grudged everything they had to give her.

Because she felt apologetic and was also very sensitive to other people's feelings, she hated going to the farm to ask for what they required, and whenever possible sent Jacob instead.

But he had so many other things to do in the garden at this time of the year, it was essential that the vegetables they had planted should be weeded, and there were also the pigeons to be prevented from eating every leaf before it came to the table, so that he could not always be spared.

Jeremy ate the remains of the portion of cheese that had been put on the table with the last scrap of butter.

Mariota felt he should have shared it with his father, but Lord Fordcombe was still far away in his thoughts and did not seem to notice that the meal was finished without his having what constituted somewhat inadequately the last course.

He rose from the table saying:

'I shall be very busy this afternoon, Mariota, and I do not wish to be disturbed.'

'I am sure nobody will do so, Papa,' Mariota replied. 'And I am glad your book is coming along so well.'

'Not badly, not badly at all!' Lord Fordcombe replied.

He left the Dining-Room and they had heard his footsteps going down the passage.

'Who does he think is likely to disturb him?' Jeremy asked. 'If anybody paid us a visit it would be a miracle!'

Mariota did not answer and he said:

'Well, at the moment that is a blessing in disguise. As soon as you have finished clearing the table, let us go upstairs and finish choosing the clothes you will wear.'

When Mariota was ready, Jeremy having saddled the horses, brought them round to the side of the house where there was a shrubbery and where they could mount without Jacob or his wife Mrs. Brindle being able to see them.

Not that they were likely to be looking, for Mrs. Brindle was growing old, and when she had washed up the luncheon things Mariota knew she would settle herself in one of the comfortable armchairs which she had arranged for the Brindles in the kitchen and doze off to sleep in front of the fire.

The large Servants' Hall, which in the old days had held twenty or more servants for every meal, was closed and so were the sculleries with their paved floors and huge sinks and the larders with the long marble slabs on which Mariota could remember there would be big open bowls from which the cream was lifted every morning.

She recalled having it on her porridge and thinking how delicious it was, but cream was another luxury they seldom had these days.

The milk they fetched from the farm was only just enough for breakfast and for tea.

'Everything is a struggle,' Mariota thought.

And yet, however difficult it might seem, she knew that what Jeremy was planning now was wrong and very risky.

Because she was so apprehensive she started to pray that there would be no coaches that afternoon on the road towards which Jeremy was leading the way.

It was in fact quite likely that the only passers-by would

be farmers in gigs, a Parson with a hearse or a wagon carrying goods from one farm to another.

There was, however, no point in saying so, and she rode a little way behind Jeremy thinking that if she had any money to spend it would be on a well-bred, spirited horse on which she could hunt in the winter.

Firefly was old, and no one would call him spirited. In fact, he usually plodded along at the pace which suited him best, and Mariota was afraid if they had to escape in a hurry, she and Firefly would be very easily captured.

Jeremy was riding the best horse they had, which was not saying much.

Their father had managed to buy Rufus cheap from a local farmer, and while he had served them well he was certainly not much to look at and no amount of training could make him jump a hedge that was more than two foot high.

But at least he had four legs and they could ride him. Mariota tried to tell herself that she must count her blessings, for the day might come when she and Jeremy would have to walk.

They reached the Worcester Road, which was a pretentious name for a dusty lane which ran through high hedgerows interspersed with small woods with trees growing right down to the roadside.

Mariota knew it was in one of these that Jeremy intended to hide and wait for a carriage to appear.

She wondered if they would have a long wait. One blessing was that the horses were quite prepared to stay quiet and were certainly not restless, as better bred animals would have been in the same circumstances.

'I wonder how long we shall have to wait,' Jeremy said, and Mariota knew from the tone of his voice that he was excited.

'This is wrong . . very . . wrong,' she told herself, but there was no use in starting the argument all over again.

There was nothing she could do but help him as he wanted her to do, or else leave him to face the danger alone.

Because she loved her brother she knew that she could

24

not bear to stay at the house waiting to hear if he was either wounded, killed or imprisoned.

At least whatever happened, they would be together, and she wondered despairingly how her father and Lynne would manage without her.

She knew her mother would have been deeply shocked at her taking part in such an escapade, and because she was frightened Mariota prayed fervently that Jeremy would find the money he wanted and they could go home in safety.

'There is somebody coming,' he said in a whisper.

Mariota felt her heart leap as she looked up the road to where she could see something moving.

The lane twisted and turned and nearly a minute passed before they were able to see more than just the roof of a vehicle above the hedges.

Then as they were aware that there was a single horse and carriage coming towards them, she held her breath, until as it drew nearer she heard Jeremy say disgustedly:

'It is only that saddler from Evesham. I am surprised he is delivering as far as this.'

'Perhaps he is taking something to the Grange,' Mariota answered. 'Lynne did say the Squire had bought some new horses at a sale.'

'He can afford them!' Jeremy said bitterly.

As the saddler passed them they could see his name inscribed on the side of his van.

'One thing we do not have to buy,' Jeremy said, 'is bridles, saddles and stirrups. We have room in the stables for forty horses, and that is the number Grandpapa kept at one time.'

Mariota thought that what they were left with now was too obvious to be spoken aloud, and because she did not wish her brother to brood over what had happened through no fault of his own she looked up the road.

Then she exclaimed:

'There *is* something coming!'

Jeremy turned his head sharply and after a moment he said:

'You are right, and I am sure there are two horses!'

There was a breathless wait until, sure enough, at the end

of the road two horses appeared moving at quite a good pace, and with a sinking of her heart Mariota knew by the way the afternoon sun glinted on their bridles that their owner was probably a wealthy man.

There was a coachman and beside him a footman on the box, and as they drew nearer Mariota could see their top-hats were embellished with cockades and the coachman's driving-coat had several tiers over the shoulders.

She was sure the carriage was as impressive as the horses, and knowing this was what Jeremy had been hoping for, she felt her heart beating so violently that it was impossible to breathe.

Then as the carriage drew near and still nearer, Mariota knew that Jeremy was as tense as she was until when the horses were only a few yards from them he rode boldly into the centre of the road.

He did not have to speak. The mask over his eyes and the pistol in his hand made the coachman draw in his horses sharply while the footman put up both his hands in a gesture of surrender.

This, Mariota knew, was what Jeremy had told her was the dangerous moment.

If the gentleman in the coach had a pistol with him he could fire out of the window without being in any danger himself, and she had therefore to go to the side of the coach with her pistol in her hand.

Because she was already anticipating what she might see she was relieved when she found that there was nobody in the carriage except for a Lady.

'Keep your hands up!' Jeremy ordered in a voice that he made deliberately authoritative and commanding.

He came round to the side of the coach and said to Mariota:

'Take over!'

She pointed her pistol not at the window of the coach, but at the servants on the box as he leaned down and opened the door.

Because she was so afraid and the pistol was trembling in her hand, Mariota did not take her eyes off the two men who seemed almost as if they were turned to stone.

The footman in particular, who was quite young, was pale with fright.

He held his arms higher and higher as if sure he would be shot at any moment.

Mariota could hear the murmur of Jeremy's voice and knew he was ordering the occupant of the carriage to hand over her money and her jewels.

Then he stepped back to say:

'Thank you, Madam.'

As he spoke he closed the carriage-door.

'Drive on,' he commanded, 'and do not look back or it will be the worse for you!'

The coachman needed no further bidding, and whipping up his horses he moved away at a far quicker pace than he had approached them earlier.

Mariota gave a sigh of relief and Jeremy said:

'A splendid haul! We can go home now and count the spoils.'

As he spoke he put his left foot in the stirrup ready to leap into the saddle and as he did so, Mariota saw with a feeling of horror a man on a horse appear through the trees on the other side of the road.

Then as she gasped and opened her lips to warn Jeremy she saw the stranger draw a pistol from his pocket and level it at her brother's back.

Without really thinking, acting on instinct rather than thought, she screamed: 'Look out!' to Jeremy and at the same time pulled the trigger of her pistol.

She did not bother to aim it, she just shot in an effort to save him.

The noise of the explosion made both Firefly and Rufus start, and it prevented Jeremy from mounting.

It also had a great effect on the stranger's horse which reared up violently, and because the action was so unexpected and he had only one hand holding the reins the rider fell backwards onto the ground and the horse, bucking, galloped off down the road.

The rider was lying motionless on the ground and Mariota now controlling Firefly with both hands, asked in a horrified whisper:

'Have I . . k. killed him?'

'I do not think you touched him,' Jeremy said, 'but we have to be sure.'

Mariota dismounted and Firefly immediately began to crop the grass by the side of the road and she knew he would not wander away.

She hurriedly followed Jeremy who was kneeling beside the fallen man.

'Have I . . wounded him?' she asked.

'No, there is not a scratch on him,' Jeremy answered, 'but he hit his head when he fell on a stone and is unconscious.'

There was a large boulder against which the rider's head was lying, and the position in which he lay showed only too clearly that he had fallen against it.

'What shall we do?' Mariota asked.

'I suppose we cannot leave him here?'

'No, no,' Mariota cried, 'he might die, and it would be our fault.'

While her brother had been speaking to her astonishment he put his hand into the inside pocket of the man's coat and pulled out a notecase.

'What are you doing?' she asked in horror.

'If he was about to fire at the Highwaymen, they would obviously rob him when he fell off his horse.'

'But you . . cannot do . . that!'

'I can as a Highwayman,' Jeremy replied. 'Then as Good Samaritans we will come to his rescue, and take him up to the house where he can stay until he recovers his senses.'

Mariota stared at him incredulously, then she understood that what he was saying was, in a twisted sort of way, common sense.

Of course, a Highwayman would not allow a rich man, which this gentleman appeared to be, to lie unconscious by the roadside without picking his pockets.

It was also quite obviously the right thing to do to take somebody who was injured to the nearest house until he was well enough to continue his journey.

Having taken the wallet out of the gentleman's coat, Jeremy was now emptying the pockets of his breeches and he appeared to be carrying quite a considerable amount of money.

Then he pulled off his mask and without him telling her to do so, Mariota did the same.

'Now,' he said, 'I found when I was taking my afternoon ride that a criminal attack had been made on a stranger riding through my land.'

'I must still ask you how we can get him back to the house?'

'It is not a question of "we",' Jeremy said. 'Nobody must see you dressed like that. Go home as quickly as you can, change and be ready to seem extremely surprised when I return with a fallen warrior on a gate.'

'You cannot carry him yourself.'

'I know that,' Jeremy said impatiently. 'I saw two men working in Robinson's field as we rode here.'

He looked down at the stranger and Mariota followed his eyes and for the first time she realised that it was a very handsome man lying at their feet.

He was exquisitely dressed, his riding-boots were smarter than any she had seen before, while his cravat was tied in an elegant fashion that she was sure her brother would try to copy.

His high hat, which had fallen off when he fell, was also a different shape from the ones her father and Jeremy wore, and she knew that everything about him was exceedingly smart, elegant and very costly.

'Hurry, Mariota!' Jeremy said sharply. 'Somebody might come by, and whatever happens you must not be seen dressed like that.'

'No . . of course . . not,' Mariota replied.

She went down into the road, mounted Firefly without any difficulty and rode him through the wood.

It was only as she hurried back to the house as quickly as he condescended to carry her that she fully realised how reprehensible and terrifying Jeremy's action had been.

But at least it was an adventure, and now they would both have something else to think about besides their lack of money.

29

CHAPTER TWO

Waiting at the house for Jeremy to bring back the stranger, Mariota thought that the minutes seemed to drag by and she was frightened that something had upset his plans.

As she thought it over she realised he had been quite right in saying they must bring the fallen man back to the house as an act of kindness.

They must have been seen by the two men working in the fields. They would have thought it very strange if she and Jeremy had ridden home without being aware that an accident had occurred.

'Jeremy is clever, and has thought it out very carefully,' Mariota told herself.

At the same time she was still horrified that he should have done anything so wrong and so dangerous.

Supposing she had not seen the stranger coming through the trees, or had not intervened, then it might be Jeremy who was lying wounded or dead, and the horror and scandal it would have caused was horrifying even to contemplate.

'We must never . . never do such a . . thing again,' Mariota told herself.

She was however afraid that since Jeremy had been successful he might think it an easy way of obtaining money.

'It is wrong, I know it is wrong, Mama,' she said silently to her mother. 'At the same time, he is young, and he does hate looking old-fashioned and having nothing to do.'

She had shut her eyes as she spoke to her mother as if she

was praying, and when she opened them again she could see through the front door that there were men coming up the drive.

As they drew nearer she could see they were Farmer Robinson's two sons who had returned from the War, one of them having received a leg wound which made him limp.

They were carrying the stranger on a gate, and as he was obviously very heavy they were moving slowly.

Mariota went to the window and watched them from behind one of the curtains which she noticed automatically had a torn lining, and the brocade which had once been a deep crimson was now faded to a pale pink.

It seemed to her that the two men took an immeasurable time to come up the slight incline towards the house where the weeds were sprouting through the gravel and the grass that had once been regularly mown had now turned itself from a lawn into a field.

Then as they reached the bottom of the steps which led up to the front door she went to meet them.

'What has happened?' she asked in a tone of well simulated surprise.

'Master Jeremy tells us to bring 'im 'ere, Miss,' one of Farmer Robinson's sons replied. 'He 'ad a fall on the road, an' Master Jeremy's gon to search fer 'is 'orse.'

Mariota looked down at the man on the gate, and she could see now there was an ugly mark on his temple where he had hit the stone, and she thought also that his shoulder was hunched in a strange way.

As if she had asked the question the man said:

'Master Jeremy thinks 'e's broke 'is collar-bone.'

'Oh, dear!' Mariota exclaimed. 'We shall have to send for Dr. Dawson. Do either of you know where he is likely to be?'

They shook their heads and Mariota said:

'We will find him later. Carry the gentleman carefully up the stairs and I will go ahead and show you in which bedroom you can put him.'

She had already decided this while changing her clothes.

When she decided to shut up most of the house she had

thought it more convenient if they were as close to each other as possible.

This meant that as she would not have thought of turning her father out of the Master Suite, the rest of them must sleep in the State Rooms.

She had therefore moved into her mother's room which was next to her father's, and Lynne was allocated the 'Queen's Room' where Queen Elizabeth had stayed when she came to the house.

It was then she had decreed that it should be called 'Queen's Ford' because the owner of the day had built a special bridge for Her Majesty over a stream which until then had always had to be forded to reach the village.

The next room to the Queen's Room, which was known as 'The King's Room' because Charles II had stayed there after the Restoration, should have been Jeremy's, but because the bed was carved with a profusion of cupids, crowns and doves, he had said it was far too fancy for him.

He preferred a more austere room on the other side of the passage where he brought together all the sporting pictures of his ancestors to cover the walls, and added his own guns because Mariota was closing the Gun-Room.

Now she led the way to the King's Room but realised as she reached it, that it would be impossible for the men to get the gate through the door.

They were sweating from having carried their heavy load up the stairs, and they set the unconscious man down on the floor.

As they did so Lord Fordcombe came from the Master Suite with a book in his hand.

He looked in astonishment at what was happening in the passage and asked:

'Who is this? And why have you brought this man here?'

'I was just going to tell you, Papa,' Mariota replied. 'Jeremy found this stranger injured on the road, having fallen from his horse, and he had him brought here for us to look after him, until he regains consciousness.'

'He has obviously hit his forehead,' Lord Fordcombe said, leaning over the prostrate man.

'Master Jeremy thinks 'e's also broke 'is collar-bone, M'Lord,' one of the men said.

'Then we had better get him to bed,' Lord Fordcombe replied, 'I will give you a hand. Will you, Mariota, tell Jacob to slip down to the village and find Dr. Dawson, unless Jeremy has already gone for him?'

'Jeremy has gone in search of the stranger's horse.'

'Then you had better send Jacob, or better still, go your-self on Firefly. It will be quicker.'

'Yes, of course, Papa.'

Mariota hurried away down the corridor, thinking as she did so that her father had taken the situation very calmly, and as there were now three men to get the stranger into bed she was not wanted.

She was glad being in such a hurry to take off Jeremy's outgrown clothes, that she had not unsaddled Firefly, but had just put him in a stall knowing there would be plenty of time to see to him later.

She took him out into the yard, stood on a mounting-block and seated herself comfortably in the saddle being careful not to tear her gown.

She and Lynne often rode without changing into a riding-habit, but as it was almost impossible for either of them ever to have new gowns, they took the greatest care with those they had, however old they might be.

Because Firefly refused to hurry since he had already been out once that afternoon, it took her nearly a quarter-of-an-hour, to reach Dr. Dawson's house, and the same time to return.

As she had expected, he was not at home, but Mrs. Dawson promised to give him a message the moment he returned.

'Fancy your brother finding an injured man on one of our roads!' Mrs. Dawson exclaimed. 'I wonder who he is? It's not often we have such excitement around here.'

'That is true,' Mariota smiled, 'and when we find out who he is, I will tell Dr. Dawson to tell you his name.'

'I shall be curious,' Mrs. Dawson said. 'He might be somebody going to stay with Lord Dudley or the Earl of

Coventry, or even the Duke of Madresfield. Does he look the type of person they would have as a guest?'

'I think so,' Mariota answered, 'but I only saw him for a moment before Papa sent me to find Doctor Dawson.'

'Oh, well, we'll know more later,' Mrs. Dawson said with relish. 'My husband tells me nothing about his patients, so I'll have to rely on you.'

Mariota laughed and rode back to the house.

As she put Firefly in his stall she knew that Jeremy was back because in the next stall which they had not used for a long time was the most magnificent stallion she had ever seen.

Jeremy had taken off the bridle and saddle, and the stallion's black coat gleamed in the sunshine coming through the window.

Mariota knew he was a horse she would love to ride, and wondered if it would be possible to do so.

Then she told herself that if anybody was going to exercise the stallion while its owner was ill, it would be Jeremy.

Excited by what was happening she ran to the house as quickly as she could.

She found her father and Jeremy in the hall.

'Is Dr. Dawson coming?' Lord Fordcombe asked.

'I left a message for him, Papa. Mrs. Dawson thinks he will be home in about half-an-hour.'

Before her father could reply she said to Jeremy:

'I see you found the stranger's horse. The man told me you were looking for him.'

'I caught him with some difficulty,' Jeremy replied, 'and rode him home. It was easier to lead Rufus.'

The way he spoke and the expression in his eyes told Mariota it had been an exciting experience, and something he had greatly enjoyed.

Her father turned towards his Study.

'Come and tell me when Dr. Dawson arrives,' he said. 'I have a lot of work to do, and all these interruptions are very disturbing.'

'I am sorry, Papa,' Mariota said.

But she did not think her father heard her and when they

34

heard the Study door close she looked at Jeremy and saw that his eyes were twinkling.

'Now we can count our ill-gotten gains,' he said. 'Come on, Mariota!'

He ran up the stairs two at a time, and she hastily ran after him.

When they were in his bedroom, although there was not the slightest chance of their being interrupted, he locked the door before he drew out of his pocket the wallet he had taken from the stranger's coat, the coins that had been in his breeches pocket, and a very pretty black handbag embroidered with white flowers.

'Oh, Jeremy, you took the lady's handbag!' Mariota exclaimed reproachfully.

'I left her a diamond ring.'

'That was generous of you!' she said a little sarcastically. 'But why?'

'She told me it was of great sentimental value, and had been given to her by her husband who was now dead.'

'Do you think she was telling you the truth?'

'I am sure she was,' Jeremy replied, 'and when she said that, I not only believed her, I also felt sorry for her.'

The way he spoke made Mariota bend forward to kiss his cheek.

'I love you!' she said. 'You are not as bad as you make yourself out to be.'

Jeremy opened the wallet and both he and Mariota stared at it incredulously. There were two notes of £100 each and three of £50!

Jeremy gave a low whistle as if it was the only way he could express his feelings.

Then he emptied the contents of the lady's black bag onto the bed and found three gold coins each of the value of £5 and ten gold sovereigns.

Mariota was past saying anything. She only stared and when Jeremy had counted the sovereigns he had taken from the stranger's pocket he said in a voice that was more surprised than elated:

'£375.'

'I cannot believe it!' Mariota said. 'Oh, Jeremy, I am sure you ought to give it back.'

'And put a rope around my neck?' he asked. 'Do not be foolish, Mariota. I have no wish to die at the moment.'

'No . . of course not . . but . . '

'There are no "buts" about it,' he said. 'There is nothing we can do but keep what has happened a complete and utter secret between us two. But I will promise you one thing.'

'What is that?'

'It is something I will never do again.'

Because she felt so relieved the tears came into Mariota's eyes, but she had to ask:

'Why . . not?'

'Because I know that I could not only have lost my own life, but put yours also at risk. As you were directly in the line of fire you could easily have been killed.'

There was an expression on Jeremy's face that Mariota had never seen before as he said:

'I realised when you fired at him and he fell off his horse the risks I had taken and what a fool I had been.'

Because she was moved the tears overflowed in Mariota's eyes and she hastily wiped them away.

'I am so . . glad you have told me . . that.'

'I thought over what had happened when I was trying to find the stranger's horse,' Jeremy went on, 'and I think, Mariota, I grew up. I certainly realised that if you had been killed I would never have been able to hold up my head again.'

'Oh, Jeremy . . Jeremy!' Mariota cried in a broken little voice.

Now because she knew her brother hated tears and was embarrassed by them with great difficulty she forced a smile to her lips.

'Well, at least,' she said, 'you will now be able to have the clothes . . you want, and go to . . London.'

'I will do that,' Jeremy said, 'but not exactly for the same reasons which made me plan what I thought of as an adventure.'

Mariota looked at him for an explanation and he said:

'I tried to think out every detail of what we should do and how we should do it, but my arrangements have obviously been upset by having this injured man on our hands.'

'I am sure Dr. Dawson will soon get him well.'

'That is not the point,' Jeremy said quickly. 'It is quite obvious that he was related in some way to the lady in the carriage, or was at any rate with her as an escort.'

'I never thought of that!' Mariota exclaimed.

'I have,' Jeremy said, 'and as it seems likely that he will be here for some days she will doubtless come in search of him and the one person she must not see is me!'

'You mean . . she might . . recognise you?' Mariota asked in dismay.

She remembered as she spoke how she herself had thought because Jeremy was so tall, broad-shouldered and, even with a mask on his face, handsome, it would be difficult for anybody to forget him.

As she grasped the whole point of what he was saying she gave a little cry.

'Of course you must go away at once!'

'That is what I thought of doing,' he said, 'and if, which is very unlikely, the stranger is still here when I come back, then by that time his wife, or whoever the lady is, is very unlikely to connect me with a badly dressed, masked Highwayman.'

'Yes, of course. You are talking absolute sense,' Mariota agreed. 'Within a week or so she will find it difficult to remember exactly what happened. At least it will not be so vivid in her mind.'

'That is what I have reasoned out,' Jeremy said, 'so if you will forgive me, Mariota, for leaving you as usual to clear up the mess, I will set off for London first thing tomorrow morning.'

'Of course, dearest. I think it is the right thing to do, but you must make some excuse to Papa.'

Jeremy laughed.

'I doubt if he will even notice I am not here, and I think it would be best if you waited until he asks where I am before you tell him.'

'All right,' Mariota agreed with a little sigh. 'As you say, Papa may not even notice we are one fewer at meals!'

Almost instinctively the thought of food made her look down at the shining sovereigns on the bed.

'As soon as I reach London,' Jeremy said, 'I am going to put this money in the Bank as a fund which I shall draw on later as and when I want it. At the same time, it would be a great mistake for anybody to think locally I am "warm in the pocket".'

'Yes, of course.'

'I therefore think it would be wise,' Jeremy went on, 'to give you just five pounds for the moment, but of course later on there will be much more.'

'No!' Mariota said sharply. 'No, I do not want it! It is very kind of you, dearest, but like you, I feel that the money is not worth the risk, and I could never spend it without thinking of that terrible moment when I saw the man on horseback . . pointing his . . gun at your . . back.'

'You saved me, and it was very clever and quick of you,' Jeremy said, 'but you will just have to forget it.'

'I will accept some money for food because that will help Papa and Lynne,' Mariota said, 'but nothing else . . nothing!'

She spoke almost violently, and as if he thought it wiser not to argue Jeremy said:

'I will do exactly as you wish, but I should not let anybody know that you have any extra money. Be careful how you spend it in the village.'

Mariota gave an unsteady little laugh.

'They are so used to my having little more than six pence in my purse, they would certainly be very curious if they caught even a glint of gold!'

'Then wait until you have run up a large bill and they will think it comes from Papa. Or else go into Malvern and change it. Here are five sovereigns to keep you going until I come back.'

'You must be very careful with the rest,' Mariota said. 'It

will have to last you for a very long time.'

'I know that,' Jeremy said in a low voice, 'but if you are afraid of my going to the gaming-tables or anything stupid like that, you can forget it!'

He picked up five sovereigns from the bed and handed them to Mariota.

Just for a moment she hesitated, feeling in her imagination that they might have been red with blood.

Then she told herself she had to be practical.

With Jeremy away there would be even less food coming into the house than there was already, and with a sick man to feed she would have to buy chickens as well as extra eggs and butter.

She knew Mrs. Robinson would be very disagreeable if she asked for more than usual without paying for it.

As if Jeremy felt he had now thought of everything he went to a cupboard in his room to pull out a very worn and battered leather hold-all.

It was large enough to hold all he would require until he reached London, and light enough for him to be able to carry it without any difficulty to the cross-roads where he would wait for the Stage-Coach.

He started to pack his things and Mariota, aware that he was thinking of the new clothes he would be able to buy in London, said hastily:

'I will press your cravats and clean your boots if you will give them to me. You must look as smart as you can until your new things are ready.'

The smile on Jeremy's lips told her how much he was looking forward to being what was called 'A Tulip of Fashion'.

Then she said:

'Did you notice the stranger's clothes?'

'Of course I did.'

'I liked the way his cravat was tied.'

'So did I,' Jeremy agreed. 'Do not worry, Mariota, I know exactly what I am going to buy, and where I am going to buy it. It will be expensive, but, as you rightly pointed out, it has to last me for a very long time.'

'It will be very exciting to see you looking like a Dandy!'

'Not a Dandy!' Jeremy said scornfully. 'They are over-dressed and conceited fools, but I would not mind being called a Beau and looking very much like that gentleman you knocked out without even touching him.'

Mariota gave a little cry.

'I do not want to . . think about it. I thought I had . . killed him!'

'Forget it! If you ask me, when he comes to his senses he will not wish to remember that he was thrown from his own horse!'

Mariota gave an unsteady little laugh, then she unlocked the door and ran across the passage to her own room.

She put the five sovereigns Jeremy had given her into one of the drawers of the dressing-table where she remembered her mother always placed the jewellery she wore, and thought once again that it was tainted money.

However, it had brought Jeremy good luck, doing no harm to anybody apart from the man in the room next door, and she thought she ought to go and look at him to see how he was.

She went into the King's Bedroom and saw that he was undressed and wearing one of her father's nightshirts. He was lying on his back almost flat on the bed.

He was, as Mariota had thought before, handsome with a clear-cut, rather hard face and a mouth which even in repose looked, she thought, cynical and as if he was extremely authoritative.

The wound on his forehead had been bleeding slightly and had spread to the centre above his eyes. By tomorrow she knew, it would be a very unpleasant dark bruise.

Because he was lying so still he looked almost as if he was carved in stone on one of the tombs which almost filled the small Church in the Park which had been built at the same time as Queen's Ford.

They were the tombs of her ancestors, and some of them, Mariota thought, were very fine and noble-looking and in a way very much like the man lying on the bed.

'I am sure he is of great importance,' she thought, and

wondered if he would be very angry when he came back to consciousness and realised what had happened to him.

Then she had a sudden fear that he might die without opening his eyes again, and it would be her fault.

Because she was so frightened at the idea she put out her hand and moving the sheets a little, laid it over his heart.

For a moment she thought he was in fact dead, then she could feel his heart beating, and it gave her a feeling of relief.

She put the sheet back over him and going to the window through which the setting sun was still shining she pulled the curtains until they dimmed the room.

Then as she walked back towards the bed it struck her that it was somehow appropriate that the man who looked so distinguished should be in the King's Room and might almost be a King himself.

As she stood beside him once again she said in her heart:

'Please God . . make him better quickly . . and let there be no lasting . . effects from his . . fall.'

It was a prayer which came from her heart.

Then quickly, almost as if she was shy, she went from the King's Room closing the door behind her.

. . . .

'I do not think there is anything seriously wrong with your patient, Miss Forde,' Dr. Dawson said as he and Mariota walked down the stairs. 'At the same time, one should never take chances with a head injury, and it might be something worse than just a bruise and what is undoubtedly a severe concussion.'

'Do you mean his brain might be affected?' Mariota asked with a tremor in her voice.

'I hope not, I sincerely hope not,' Dr. Dawson replied, 'but quite frankly, I would like a second opinion, and there is a Physician in Worcester for whom I have the greatest respect.'

'Then perhaps it would be best to send for him,' Mariota said in a low voice.

She was thinking as she spoke that of course the stranger

41

would be able to pay for such an extravagance, while in the past they had found it difficult to meet the very small fees that Dr. Dawson charged for attending them when they were ill.

'And what about his . . collar-bone?' she asked.

'It is not broken,' the Doctor replied, 'but he may have cracked a bone. He certainly will have a very bruised shoulder as well as a bruised head.'

'I think you must tell Papa about him,' Mariota said. 'In fact he asked to be informed as soon as you arrived, and I forgot about it.'

Dr. Dawson smiled.

'I will not disturb your father any more than I can help. How is his book progressing?'

'I think he is half-way through it,' Mariota replied, 'but as there have been so many Fordes and they have done so many things over the centuries, it is likely to go into several volumes.'

'It keeps your father happy,' Dr. Dawson said, 'and that is a better tonic than anything I can prescribe.'

He laughed at his own joke and walked towards the Study.

Mariota ran to the kitchen to fetch the bottle of sherry that was kept for when her father had a visitor.

It was not a bottle they had bought themselves, but had been a present with several bottles of port from the Squire last Christmas. After they had finished the first bottle Lord Fordcombe had said to Jeremy:

'I think what we have left must be kept for special occasions. It always makes me extremely embarrassed not to have any refreshment to offer any friend who comes to the house, but wine is something I am well aware we cannot afford.'

Jeremy sighed.

'I quite agree with you, Papa. At the same time it is a very good port, and I have enjoyed drinking it.'

'So have I,' Lord Fordcombe agreed, 'and I do not mind telling you, Jeremy, that I often long for a glass of claret, and it is depressing to think that our cellars are empty.'

When everything had to be sold to meet the previous Lord Fordcombe's debts, his stock of choice wines had realised a considerable sum but it had left the spendthrift's son and grandson very thirsty.

Mariota placed the decanter of sherry which she noticed was only half full and two small glasses onto a silver salver she had fortunately cleaned only three days ago, and hurried to the Study.

Her father looked up and said: 'Thank you, my dear,' as she set it down beside him and added: 'I am sure, Dawson, you will join me.'

'I shall be delighted to do so, My Lord,' Dr. Dawson replied, and Mariota slipped away to wait for the Doctor until he was ready to leave.

When he joined her in the hall he said:

'I am well aware, Miss Forde, that the nursing of your unexpected guest rests on you, and I am afraid I must ask you to sit up with him tonight in case he should become restless. Your father says that he and Jacob can manage to look after him in the daytime.'

Mariota did not reply, but she knew that her father would soon grow bored with having to help in the sickroom, and it would be difficult for Jacob to stay there for very long when he had so many other things to do.

'I will manage,' she said, 'and I am sure his friends or relatives will soon come looking for him.'

'I am sure they will,' Dr. Dawson said consolingly, 'but since we have no way of ascertaining who they may be, there is nothing we can do in the meantime.'

When he walked down the steps to where his gig drawn by a tired horse was waiting, he added:

'I will send to Worcester for Dr. Mortimer, and I will call first thing tomorrow, so do not worry.'

'I will try not to,' Mariota promised and waved as he drove away.

She was thinking as she went back up the stairs how she could make herself comfortable on the sofa in the King's Room, and as she was a very light sleeper, she knew she would be able to get a little sleep besides listening for the unconscious man.

'He is obviously going to be a great deal of trouble,' she thought, 'at the same time, we have nobody to blame but ourselves.'

. . . .

Jeremy left early the next morning to catch the Stage Coach which passed the crossroads at the end of the village at about six-thirty.

It would take him two long days to reach London, but he was in such high spirits that Mariota knew that even the journey would seem amusing.

He had placed his precious money very carefully in his pockets, and had hidden none of it in his bag.

It sometimes happened that while the passengers from the Stage Coach were eating inside a Posting Inn, thieves would rifle the baggage.

Mariota knew too from the conversations she had heard in the past that there was always the chance of travellers being robbed at night, and she impressed upon Jeremy that even to save money it would be unwise for him to share a room at an Inn.

'I have thought of that,' he said. 'Do not worry, Mariota. Having got this money the hard way, I am not going to lose or spend foolishly a single penny of it.'

He had given her a warm hug as he had kissed her good-bye, and said:

'Thank you for being the most wonderful sister anyone could have. I only hope that when the stranger wakes up he will be more amusing than he is at present!'

Mariota laughed but when she went upstairs she thought that in a way he could be said to be amusing her in a manner she could not explain to her family.

Because she had been so much alone while she dusted and tidied the house, she had got in the way of telling herself stories, which sometimes seemed so exciting and so interesting that she thought if she had time she ought to write them down.

'Perhaps I might even sell them and make some money,' she thought.

But there was so much to do that it was difficult enough to find time to mend and darn her clothes as well as her father's and Jeremy's, so the stories remained in her mind.

Now the unconscious man was giving her splendid inspiration for new and exciting adventures.

She only had to look at him before she blew out the candles, leaving only a tiny night-light to guide her should he waken, to find a new and thrilling tale coming from her mind.

This was perhaps because he looked so different from any other man she had ever seen before.

He was not as handsome as her father or as good-looking and attractive as Jeremy, but it was easy to imagine him as a General leading his troops into battle and being victorious against what seemed a superior enemy.

She made him an explorer who climbed the highest peaks of the Himalayas, or who discovered a huge diamond mine which brought prosperity to a great number of poor people.

Sometimes, like Marco Polo or Christopher Columbus he discovered new worlds, or else like a Greek god from Olympus he came down to bring a light and new thought to those living in darkness.

There were so many different ways in which Mariota imagined him that it was quite a shock when on the second night of her vigil in the King's Room there was a sound from the bed which she had not heard before.

As she hastily threw off the blanket and the eiderdown with which she had covered herself, and lit a candle, she realised that her patient had become restless.

He was moving from side to side and murmuring, and she knew that now he had the fever which Dr. Mortimer had predicted might happen before he came back to consciousness.

'Most patients with concussion talk a lot of nonsense and become exceedingly restless and sometimes even violent before they revert to being normal.'

He added to re-assure her:

'Do not be alarmed, Miss Forde. It is quite usual behaviour, and if he becomes too difficult, I have left some soothing medicament which will send him back to sleep.'

Mariota listened to the doctor's warning and repeated it to Jacob who she felt even when she said it several times had not taken it all in.

Now she went to the bedside, and putting her hand on the stranger's forehead found as she had expected that it was very hot, almost burning.

As she touched him he opened his eyes and in the candle-light she could see that he was staring at her blankly.

'Where — am I? What — has — happened?'

'It is all right,' Mariota replied. 'You have had an accident, but are quite safe.'

'I am hot — too hot.'

'I know. I have a cool drink for you.'

She reached to where by the bedside there was some lemonade she had made freshly that afternoon.

She put her arm behind his head and lifted him up a little and he understood as she held the glass to his lips and drank thirstily.

'Now, please, go back to sleep,' Mariota begged. 'You will soon be well again.'

He appeared for a moment to want to argue with her, then as if it was too much effort, his eyes closed wearily and he fell asleep.

Mariota tucked in his bed clothes and went back to the sofa.

She left the candle alight in case he should wake again, seeing the outline of his dark head against the pillow she thought it strange he should have blue eyes.

She had somehow expected them to be grey like her own, although why she had no idea, but his eyes had been the deep blue of a stormy sea.

With his dark hair she thought he seemed not only unusual, but very striking.

'I wish I knew who he was,' she thought before she shut her eyes.

The next day her curiosity was rewarded.

46

She had only just finished helping Mrs. Brindle to wash up the breakfast things, and Joseph had gone upstairs to sit beside the patient until she could go and relieve him when there was the sound of carriage wheels outside the front door.

Quickly Mariota put up her hands to tidy her hair and pulled down the sleeves of her cotton gown, fastening them at the wrists.

Then as the front door bell peeled noisily she walked slowly and she hoped with dignity into the hall.

Standing on the steps was a footman wearing the same livery as the man she had held at gun-point on the box of the carriage.

'Excuse me, Ma'am,' he said politely, 'but I understands the Earl of Buckenham might be staying here.'

'The Earl of Buckenham?' Mariota repeated.

'They tells me in the village that a gentleman were found on the roadside by Mr. Jeremy Forde, and carried here on his instructions.'

'Yes, that is true,' Mariota answered.

The footman did not wait to hear any more, but ran down the steps to open the carriage door.

He said something to the occupant inside, and a lady stepped out who Mariota was certain was the same woman who Jeremy had robbed of her money in the little black bag with the white embroidery.

She was dressed in black, and as she came towards her Mariota saw that she was very attractive but not very young.

'My servant tells me,' she said in a soft, musical voice, 'that my brother the Earl of Buckenham might be staying here.'

'We did not know who your brother was,' Mariota replied, 'but he was injured and lying by the roadside.'

'Injured?' the lady exclaimed. 'Was he shot?'

Because Mariota was prepared for this question she raised her eyebrows in surprise and exclaimed:

'Shot? Why should you think that?'

'Because I was held up by Highwaymen and as the carriage drove away after I had been robbed I heard a shot,

47

but there was nothing I could do about it.'

The way she spoke told Mariota that the servants had panicked and carried her out of reach of the criminals who were threatening them, so that the lady had not realised what had occurred until her brother did not turn up at wherever they were staying.

'How very frightening for you!' Mariota said aloud. 'But, please, will you not come in? I am sure you wish to see your brother, although he is not yet fully conscious.'

'Is he badly injured?'

'No, I do not think so. He has been seen by two Doctors, and he had concussion from falling against a stone . . '

'He fell?' the lady interrupted, 'but surely, if he fell he must have been shot!'

'I do not quite know how it happened,' Mariota said, 'but I understood your brother fell from his horse and hit his head against a boulder which has inflicted a very painful bruise on his temple.'

They had reached the hall by now and the lady stood still to stare at Mariota as if she could not believe what she was hearing.

'I find it hard to understand,' she said. 'My brother is a noted horseman, and I have never in my life known him to fall for no apparent reason.'

'It is difficult to understand what happened,' Mariota answered, 'but now you tell me there were Highwaymen near the place where he was found, perhaps they shot at his horse and missed.'

'You have his horse?'

'Yes, he is in our stables, and not injured in any way.'

'I am glad to hear that,' the lady said.

'Would you like to come upstairs and see your brother?' Mariota suggested.

'Yes, yes, of course. You will understand I have been so desperately worried about him. The terrible thing is that when I reached Madresfield where we are staying with the Duke, I could not remember, and neither could my servants, where we were when the Highwaymen robbed me.'

She sighed and went on:

'Up until now, we have been looking in the wrong places, and it was only last night that one of the Duke's servants made enquiries in your village and was told that an injured man had been brought here.'

'We have been looking after your brother,' Mariota said soothingly, 'and our own Doctor and a very experienced one from Worcester have both said there is nothing really wrong with him except he is concussed.'

'And your servants have been nursing him?' the lady asked. 'How very, very kind. You must allow me to thank them.'

'As we are very short-staffed,' Mariota said with a little smile, 'I have had to do more of the nursing myself, while my father and our man-servant, who is very old, have washed and shaved him.'

'Is Lord Fordcombe your father?'

'Yes.'

'And your name is the same?'

'My name is Mariota Forde.'

'And mine is Noreen Coddington. My husband, Lord Coddington, was killed in the war, and you can imagine as I am now very much alone, how much my brother means to me.'

'Of course I understand,' Mariota replied. 'I too have a brother who means a great deal to me.'

She thought it might be a mistake to mention Jeremy, but as he was not there it could not be of any importance.

They walked along the passage to the King's Room, and as she stole a glance at Lady Coddington she thought she had a kind, gentle face, and was not the sort of person who would be aggressively determined to bring the criminals who had done her very little harm to the gallows.

They entered the King's Room and Jacob, who was sitting on a chair by the window hastily rose to his feet.

'Th' gent'man he awake, Miss Mariota,' he said, 'but 'e be quite quiet.'

'Thank you, Jacob,' Mariota said. 'I will look after him now.'

49

Delighted to be relieved of his duties Jacob shuffled away and Lady Coddington moved to the bed to look down at her brother.

'I am here, Alvic, and I am so very, very glad to have found you,' Mariota heard her say. 'How are you? Are you in pain?'

'A — little,' the Earl said slowly as if to speak was an effort. 'I cannot — remember what — happened.'

'I will tell you when you are better,' Lady Coddington said. 'I am sure now you must rest and sleep and not worry about anything.'

'I am — very — tired.'

The words came with an effort from between the Earl's lips, and as his eyes closed his sister moved away from the bedside.

As if she thought their voices might disturb the Earl, Mariota walked out of the room into the passage and Lady Coddington followed her before she said:

'It is a terrible bruise!'

'I know,' Mariota replied, 'but his head hit a very large stone, and I believe there is another bruise almost as bad on his shoulder.'

'He is alive — that is all that matters — and those wicked men did not shoot him, as they might have done.'

'He had no other injuries,' Mariota said quickly.

There was a little silence. Then Lady Coddington said:

'Do you think it would be possible to speak to your father? I feel I must thank him for having my brother here, and of course as soon as I get back to Madresfield I will send over my brother's valet to help nurse him.'

'I am sure it will be pleasant for His Lordship to have his own valet with him,' Mariota agreed.

'It has been very kind of you to look after him,' Lady Coddington said. 'You will find that Hicks is an excellent nurse, and has been with my brother since his Army days and is, I promise you, no trouble about the house.'

She spoke in a way which told Mariota she had understood how few servants they had at Queen's Ford.

She would in fact have been very unobservant if she had

50

not realised that the carpets were threadbare and the curtains faded, and it was obvious that everything about the home was poverty-stricken.

As they walked down the staircase towards her father's Study, Mariota felt a pride which told her they were not prepared to be criticised by anybody.

They had done their best, and if their best was not good enough, then the Earl of Buckenham could be taken somewhere else.

She opened the door of the Study, and as her father looked up from his desk where he was writing and frowned at being disturbed she said quickly:

'Lady Coddington has come here, Papa, to identify our injured guest as her brother, the Earl of Buckenham. She is also very anxious to meet you.'

'I am indeed!' Lady Coddington said.

She walked across the room with her hand outstretched.

'Thank you, thank you, Lord Fordcombe, for being so kind as to look after my brother. I can never be sufficiently grateful to you.'

'I am glad my son found him,' Lord Fordcombe replied. 'It might have been fatal for him to have lain where he was all night. But fortunately he was carried back here, and my daughter has nursed him, I think, most efficiently.'

'You have all been so very kind,' Lady Coddington said, 'and I feel most apologetic that we have imposed on your hospitality.'

Mariota saw her father smile and looking very handsome as he did so, and she thought he was pleased at the way in which Lady Coddington was thanking him.

'May I offer you a glass of sherry?' he asked.

'That would be very pleasant,' Lady Coddington replied.

Mariota went quickly from the room to fetch the decanter.

By now, as her father had given a glass to Dr. Mortimer as well as to Dr. Dawson, there was only very little sherry left.

She wondered if she should go down to the cellars and

51

find another of the prized bottles, then decided it would take too long.

Instead she carried it in on the salver as she had done before to find her father and Lady Coddington sitting in front of the fireplace discussing not the Earl of Buckenham, but her father's work on the family history.

'Now I remember,' Lady Coddington was saying. 'I have heard of Queen's Ford, and always thought it such an attractive name, and of course I have read of your ancestors in the history books. You must be very proud of your family.'

'I am very proud of their exploits as soldiers, sailors and politicians,' Lord Fordcombe answered. 'I just wish at times they had not found it so expensive to serve their country. This generation came into the world with nothing, and they will go out the same way!'

Lady Coddington laughed.

'You make me feel guilty because my husband's relatives, the Coddingtons, did the opposite. They are not as old a family as yours, but they always seemed to winkle themselves into positions of power and found it very much to their advantage.'

'Then they were much more fortunate than we have been,' Lord Fordcombe replied, and appeared to think it amusing.

Because she was curious to see how his sister's visit had affected the Earl, Mariota left them and went upstairs.

As she had half-expected, his eyes were open, and as she approached the bed said:

'Was Noreen — here just — now?'

'Yes, your sister came to see you. She has been looking for you, and now she has found you.'

'And — who are — you?'

'My name is Mariota Forde.'

'Mariota. I have not — heard that — name — before.'

'You must go to sleep,' Mariota said gently, 'and get well quickly. Your sister wants you back on your feet, but she is very happy to have found you.'

The Earl did not reply, but Mariota knew he was

watching her as she tidied the bedroom and picked up the jug of lemonade that was almost empty.

'Would you like a little more to drink?' she asked. 'And I think tonight you will be able to eat something.'

'I am — not hungry but — thirsty.'

Mariota poured out what was left in the jug and realised as she did so that the honey with which she had sweetened the lemonade had sunk to the bottom of it, and wondered if the Earl would find it distasteful.

She did not say anything and he drank it without protest. When he laid his head back on the pillows, she said:

'I am going downstairs now, to say goodbye to your sister. Then I will come back again. You are quite certain you do not want anything?'

'You will — come — back?'

'I promise you I will. I am looking after you until your valet arrives tomorrow.'

He did not answer and she wondered if he had understood.

Then as she reached the door and looked back she saw that his eyes were still on her and thought perhaps he was afraid of being left alone.

'I will not be long,' she promised, and had the feeling that was what he wanted to hear.

CHAPTER THREE

The Earl's bedroom was opened by Hicks, and Mariota carried in a large vase filled with flowers.

'I thought these would cheer you up,' she said as she set them down on a table where the Earl could see them from the bed.

'I certainly need something,' he replied in the dry manner she had come to learn was characteristic of him.

She looked at him questioningly and he said:

'I am feeling rather neglected. You have not been to see me this morning.'

'I am sorry,' Mariota replied, 'but I thought as you had your valet with you that you would not want me.'

'Hicks, while admirable in many ways,' the Earl replied, 'is not the most interesting of conversationalists.'

The valet had left the room as soon as Mariota entered it, and now, having arranged the flowers, she walked to stand beside the bed looking at the Earl, and thinking how much better he seemed.

The bruise on his forehead was almost black and it gave him a somewhat strange appearance, but at the same time, the colour had come back into his face.

With his hair brushed back from his broad forehead, he looked very different from the way he had when he had lain unconscious and she thought he might be dead.

She was aware that his nightshirt which was of silk was very much smarter than her father's which he had worn at first.

His own had a high frilled collar which looked almost like a cravat, and sitting up against the pillows he appeared to have an authority which she had sensed long before he spoke to her.

'This afternoon,' she said, 'your sister will be coming here again to see you, and Papa is going to show her some of the older parts of the house which are now locked up.'

'Why?' the Earl enquired.

'I should have thought that was obvious,' Mariota replied. 'We cannot afford to keep them open because they would have to be cleaned, and there is nobody but me and old Jacobs to do the work, who you know is not a streak of lightning.'

She spoke lightly because she was trying to amuse the Earl, but she saw there was a slight frown between his eyes as he asked:

'Are you so very poor?'

'Worse than the Church mice!' Mariota smiled.

There was a little silence. Then the Earl said:

'I realise I am being an encumbrance, and as the Doctors refuse to allow me to move, you must tell me what I can do about it.'

Dr. Dawson had been very firm when he had said the Earl was not to be moved until the crack in his shoulder had healed, and the headaches from which he suffered every day ceased.

'We are quite happy to do what we can for you,' Mariota said quickly, 'and you must not listen to Lynne.'

The Earl smiled.

Lynne had been very frank when he was well enough to be allowed to see her.

'You have certainly brought the first bit of excitement we have had in the neighbourhood since the last important person occupied this room!' she had said.

The Earl raised his eyebrows and she explained:

'That was Charles II, and now I think about it, you are rather like him.'

'Thank you,' the Earl replied.

'Papa has a whole chapter in his book of the feasting and merry-making there was at Queen's Ford when he came here, but unfortunately your feasting will consist of rabbit and more rabbit!'

She saw the surprise in the Earl's face as she explained:

'It is the only free food available at this time of the year, and Jeremy has often said that if he had to eat rabbit again he will grow a bushy tail!'

The Earl laughed.

'I can see it is a very sad story.'

'Of course it is, for us,' Lynne replied. 'I expect you have the most scrumptious dishes in your house in Oxfordshire.'

'Who has been talking to you about my house?' the Earl enquired.

'Elaine. That is the girl with whom I share lessons,' Lynne replied. 'She told me how important you are, and that you live in great luxury almost as if you were Royal, and all the lovely ladies who do not already have husbands are trying to marry you.'

The Earl tried to look severe and failed. Instead he smiled and said:

'I can see my reputation has preceded me.'

'Yes, even here in what my brother Jeremy calls "this dead and alive hole" and "the back of beyond", as we have no decent horses to get away from it, we just sit and watch the turnips grow.'

'You are very voluble on the subject,' the Earl remarked mockingly.

'As food is the only thing we have to think about, a diet of rabbit has undoubtedly given us rabbit brains,' Lynne retorted.

It was then that Mariota had come into the room and heard the last sentence.

'You are not to tire His Lordship,' she said sharply, 'and he is not interested in our problems.'

'I thought he would like to know how the poor and needy live,' Lynne replied.

'I doubt it,' Mariota said. 'Dearest, could you go and tidy the Drawing Room for me, before Lady Coddington arrives? You have left all your things strewn over the sofa.'

Lynne rose from the chair in which she had been sitting to say to the Earl:

'That is a polite way of getting rid of me. Very well, if

Mariota wants you to herself, I will make myself scarce.'

She gave him an engaging, very attractive smile and left the bedroom before Mariota could rebuke her.

'I am sorry,' Mariota said to the Earl when she had gone, 'if Lynne bored you with our difficulties.'

'I was not in the least bored,' the Earl replied almost sharply. 'I am just feeling embarrassed that I have forced myself upon you and brought Hicks into the house without doing anything about it.'

Because she had the uncomfortable feeling he might be going to offer her money for their keep Mariota stiffened.

As if he knew what she was thinking he said:

'I am well aware, Miss Forde, that a family which has embellished history for so many generations can be very proud, at the same time . . '

'. . at the same time, I was hoping Your Lordship would be content,' Mariota interrupted stiffly. 'And you did say that the chicken was delicious.'

'It was,' the Earl said firmly. 'But I suppose, now I think about it, that it was an extra item on the housekeeping bill.'

Mariota thought he would be very surprised if he knew it was his own money, taken by Jeremy from his pocket, which had paid for it.

The Earl went on:

'Actually I told my sister when she comes this afternoon to bring you some fruit from the Duke's greenhouses which are famous. But I think we should also be practical and suggest that tomorrow she brings dishes that will not only build up my strength, but yours as well.'

Because she did not know how to answer him, Mariota walked away from the bed to stand at the window looking out at the untidy, overgrown garden.

To her it looked very beautiful in the sunshine, but she knew to a stranger it would merely look unkempt and sadly in need of gardening.

But a pride she did not even realise she possessed was rebelling against the idea of the Earl providing for his keep, and she felt if they had to suffer after he left, then it would be a just retribution because his being here was due solely to Jermey's and her own masquerade as Highwaymen.

'Come here!' the Earl said. 'I want to talk to you, and I see no reason why I should have to raise my voice.'

He was giving her orders, Mariota thought, and she resented the fact. At the same time he was an invalid, and she could not refuse to do as he asked.

Slowly and reluctantly she walked back to the bedside and the Earl said:

'I am well aware now that your brother saved me from lying all night in the open when I might have developed pneumonia, and that you personally have nursed and looked after me, until my sister found me, at great inconvenience to yourself. If you put yourself in my place, would you also not wish to show your gratitude?'

It was difficult for Mariota to reply and he went on:

'Hicks has told me how much you do in the house *personally*, and that most of the food that has been brought up to me has been cooked by you. Do you enjoy being nothing but a servant in your own home?'

'It is something I am quite content to do,' Mariota answered defiantly.

'Nonsense,' the Earl said in a sharp voice which she realised he used when he was annoyed. 'I do not have to tell you that if you went to London you would be a sensation, and in a year's time your sister, Lynne, will be the toast of St. James's.'

Mariota gave a little sigh before she said almost as sharply as the Earl had spoken:

'If wishes were horses, beggars could ride, My Lord. As it is, we try to accept life as it is and make the best of it.'

She paused and as the Earl did not speak she added:

'I hope you will not encourage Lynne to be discontented and, since she has seen you, to yearn for the sort of amusements she will never have.'

'Are you seriously contemplating that you and Lynne will live here for ever with nothing to enliven your existence except for the occasional excitement of a stranger falling off his horse?'

Because of the scathing way in which the Earl spoke Mariota longed to reply that they had moments of wild gaiety or that a fortune was waiting for them round the corner.

Because he had upset her and she felt almost as if he was touching a sore spot she said:

'If Your Lordship . . finds Queen's Ford so . . unpleasant, I am sure in a few days the Doctors will allow you to be . . moved to the Duke's house. Then you will . . never have to . . see us or . . think of us . . again.'

She thought the Earl would snap back at her, but instead he said in a very different voice:

'Come here, Mariota!'

She noticed he used her Christian name but she did not protest. Then when she did not obey him he put out his hand to her saying:

'Come here. I want to say something to you.'

She moved closer to him and because his hand was outstretched, almost as if she was compelled to do so, she laid hers in it.

As his fingers closed, he was aware that hers were cold, and when her palm touched his there was a vibration between them that was inescapable.

His blue eyes were looking into her grey ones, as he said:

'I have hurt you, Mariota. I did not mean to do so. Forgive me.'

He spoke to her in a different manner from the way he had before and because of it, and the fact that he was holding her hand, she felt shy.

At the same time, she felt, because he was being kind, a warm response within her breast.

'I want to help you,' the Earl said, 'and while you personally wish to be independent of me, you should think of your father, your pretty sister and your brother whom I have not yet met.'

'I do . . think of . . them,' Mariota objected.

'I know you do, and I have already realised that you carry the burdens of the family on your back, but it is something which cannot go on for ever.'

'Perhaps . . something will . . happen one . . day.'

'What sort of thing?'

Because he was speaking quietly in a manner which seemed sympathetic and at the same time interested, Mariota replied:

'I tell myself stories that we will find a treasure in the attics or hidden in the ground. Or perhaps Papa's book will sell, and make us a fortune, or a Genie will appear in a cloud of smoke to grant me three wishes.'

She spoke dreamily and was not aware that the Earl was watching her eyes, or even that his fingers had tightened on hers.

'What would your three wishes be?' he asked.

'That we could restore the house to the way it looked in the past; that Jeremy could have magnificent horses like your stallion to ride, and that Lynne could go to London, and as you have said be the toast of St. James's.'

'And what would you wish for yourself?' the Earl asked.

'I think I should be happy if all those wishes were granted.'

'I think if you are honest,' he said, 'you would wish for somebody to love you, and for you to love him. That is what every woman wants.'

'I . . suppose . . so,' Mariota agreed.

She was not looking at the Earl as she spoke, but into her dreamland where she lived when she was alone and told herself stories.

'You have never been in love?' the Earl asked.

'Only in my . . dreams.'

'And what is your dream-lover like?'

'Tall, dark, very handsome, and a magnificent rider. Strong, and authoritative, and yet at the same time if anybody is in trouble, kind, considerate and understanding.'

As Mariota spoke again dreamily the words came out just as she had thought of them for so long.

Once again she was seeing the hero of her story climbing the mountains, exploring the world or, and this was one of her favourite tales, winning a race on his own horse.

She had never seen any of the great Classic Races, but she had read about them in the newspapers, and sometimes there were Steeple Chases or Point-to-Point in the County to which, if they were not too far away, Jeremy would take her.

But they were usually not very happy occasions because he was always so frustrated that he could not compete in them himself.

'I could have beaten that fellow hollow!' he would say as the winner was cheered and acclaimed after he had passed the Winning Post.

'I imagine your ideal man will be somewhat difficult to find,' the Earl said.

Because the dry note was back in his voice he brought Mariota back to reality.

Embarrassed that she had been carried away by her own thoughts she took her hand from his and said quickly:

'Your Lordship must think I am talking the most arrant nonsense, and it is only because I am so much . . alone that I . . imagine such things.'

'Will you think I am a Fortune Teller if I say that one day your dreams will come true?' the Earl asked.

'I think that is very unlikely,' Mariota replied. 'And now, I must go downstairs and help prepare your luncheon. I only hope you will find it edible.'

'Now you are being unkind to me,' the Earl said, 'and I should point out that it is hardly in keeping with your role as a ministering angel.'

'If that is what I have been,' Mariota replied, 'I think Your Lordship is almost well enough now to look after yourself without angels.'

'I very much doubt it,' the Earl said. 'As a matter of fact, if you are interested, my head is aching unpleasantly.'

Mariota gave a little exclamation of concern.

'You must lie down at once,' she said. 'It is all my fault for talking to you so much. I know Dr. Dawson when he comes tonight will be very annoyed if I tell him that I have upset you.'

'You have not upset me,' the Earl replied. 'You have only worried me a little. I hate problems I cannot solve, or obstacles I cannot demolish.'

Mariota took one of the pillows from behind his head very gently so as not to jerk him.

'Try to sleep for half an hour before I bring you your luncheon.'

'I do not want to sleep,' the Earl said obstinately. 'I want to talk to you.'

'With the best will in the world, I cannot be in two places

61

at once,' Mariota answered, 'and although Mrs. Brindle does her best for us, her cooking is not good enough for you.'

'Very well, I will let you go,' the Earl agreed, 'but will you promise to talk to me again this afternoon while your father is entertaining my sister? You must admit that is only fair.'

'I would like to talk to you, My Lord,' Mariota said, 'but it would be better for you to sleep.'

'Sleep! Sleep!' the Earl exclaimed. 'You and the Doctors seem to think it is a cure for everything. Personally, I find it far more healing to listen to you, even when you are being disagreeable to me.'

'I am not . . that is not fair . . ' Mariota began to protest, then realised that the Earl was teasing her.

His eyes met hers and for no reason she could ascertain she felt the colour rising in her cheeks.

'Please . . try to . . sleep,' she begged a little incoherently, then slipped from the room closing the door very quietly behind her.

The Earl did not close his eyes. Instead he stared across the room at the vase of flowers which Mariota had brought him.

There was syringa and white lilac, and there were also several roses which were only in bud.

The whole arrangement looked very young and spring-like and he thought the flowers were in fact representative of Mariota herself.

Then he sighed, and there was an expression in his eyes that seemed to be one of pain.

. . . .

Lady Coddington arrived at nearly twenty past three and immediately went upstairs to her brother's room.

She had given up ringing the bell, knowing it was quite unnecessary for Jacob to be summoned from whatever he was doing in the kitchen to escort her upstairs.

Instead she told her footman on the carriage to carry in the fruit she had brought with her and without waiting hurried into the house.

'If I am a little late, Alvic,' she said, 'you must forgive me, but luncheon took even longer than usual, even though we started earlier. The Duke is rather inclined to drone on.'

'I am aware of that,' the Earl replied.

Lady Coddington kissed her brother's cheek, and said to Mariota who had risen from the chair in which she had been sitting by the bedside:

'Good afternoon, Miss Forde, or, please, may I call you Mariota? And because I can see my brother is looking much better than he did yesterday, you know how grateful I am to you.'

'I am afraid His Lordship had a headache again this morning,' Mariota said.

Lady Coddington looked concerned, and the Earl said quickly:

'It was nothing, and it has gone now.'

Mariota thought that was very likely untrue, but was aware he did not wish to talk about his health.

She was also thinking how lovely Lady Coddington looked. For the first time she was not wearing black, but a gown of mauve, the colour of the lilacs that were just coming into bloom in the garden.

Her bonnet was trimmed with ribbons of the same colour, round her neck was a necklace of amethysts and diamonds, and the same stones glittered on her fingers as she pulled off her gloves.

Because she thought Lady Coddington would want to be alone with her brother Mariota moved towards the door and as she reached it she said:

'I know father is looking forward to seeing you later, My Lady, and you know where to find him in the Study.'

'Yes, of course,' Lady Coddington replied, 'and as I suspect you are warning me not to overtire my brother, I promise you I will not stay too long with him.'

'Thank you.'

She went from the room and Lady Coddington said:

'What a charming girl she is, and so lovely. It is a shame that Lord Fordcombe is so poor that he is unable to go anywhere and will not accept the hospitality of the Duke or any other of the land-owners in the County.'

'Why will he not do that?' the Earl asked.

'The Duke says it is because he is too proud to be a guest and not be able to invite his host back.'

As she spoke Lady Coddington looked round the room and said:

'This is one of the loveliest houses I have ever seen! It really breaks my heart, Alvic, to see the condition it is in at the moment. There is hardly a window where there is not a pane of glass broken, and every curtain is in tatters.'

'Well, there is nothing you can do about it,' the Earl said. 'I have just been battling with Mariota because I intended to ask you tomorrow to bring over some food with you.'

'Food?' Lady Coddington exclaimed in surprise.

'They cannot afford to keep me,' the Earl said abruptly, 'and the youngest girl, who incidentally will be an outstanding beauty, informed me I am taking the bread out of their mouths.'

'I never thought of that,' Lady Coddington said. 'It is dreadful to think they are so poor when we are so rich. Surely you could persuade them . . '

'Do not waste your breath,' her brother interrupted. 'They are as proud as the Devil and the only way you can bring me food from Madresfield is to make me out to be a *gourmet* who is not satisfied with the meals I am having already.'

'And are you?' Lady Coddington asked.

The Earl pursed his lips together before he replied:

'I rather feel that I am back in the Nursery.'

His sister laughed.

'I am sure that is very good for you. I have always said your Chef's food is delicious, but too rich.'

'Then I suggest you ask the Duke's Chef for pâtés, some of the brawn for which he is famous, an ox tongue and anything else that is available at the moment.'

'But supposing that child and her father feel insulted and refuse to accept the food if it arrives here?'

'I will deal with Mariota, and if there is any difficulty with Lord Fordcombe, I will leave him to you.'

There was a smile on his sister's face which the Earl did not miss. Then he said:

'As I imagine His Lordship is waiting for you, I suggest you go to him and come back to me later. In the meantime, I will rest.'

'If you will do that I will certainly leave you,' Lady Coddington said.

She went towards the door. Then she exclaimed:

'But how foolish of me! I had forgotten to tell you that Elizabeth sends her love, and asks if she may come over here with me tomorrow.'

'No, I think that would be a mistake,' the Earl said. 'Tell her to wait until I am better. I really find that too much chatter brings on one of my headaches.'

'Of course, dearest Alvic, I understand.'

Lady Coddington went from the room leaving the Earl with a frown between his eyes, and he was still frowning when Mariota came back to see if he needed anything.

. . . .

'I am going to be frank with you, My Lord,' Dr. Mortimer said, 'and say that although you may want to get up as you have told me, and perhaps to leave Queen's Ford, it would be an extremely foolish thing to do.'

Dr. Mortimer waited to hear the Earl protest, and when he did not do so he went on:

'I am still a little worried by your headaches and the fact that the bruise has not yet begun to fade. It would in my opinion be foolhardy and might have far-reaching consequences if you do not rest until you are very much stronger than you are at the moment.'

'But I cannot stay in bed for ever!' the Earl said sharply.

'You have only been here for four days,' Dr. Mortimer replied, 'and unless you would like to have the opinion of Sir Wilfred Lawson, or another of His Majesty's Physicians, you must believe that I am thinking of your best interests when I say you must rest, My Lord, however boring it may be, until both your head and your shoulder are in very much better condition than they are at the moment.'

'It is not that I wish to leave Queen's Ford,' the Earl said, 'it is just that I dislike being in bed.'

'Very well,' Dr. Mortimer conceded, 'you may get up tomorrow and sit in a chair by the window, but in your robe, and not dressed. The moment you feel tired or your head hurts you must go back to bed. Does Your Lordship understand?'

'I understand,' the Earl said, 'and I also now understand the resentment that other people feel when I give them unwelcome orders.'

'Then it is undoubtedly very good for you,' Dr. Mortimer smiled. 'But I am still prepared, My Lord, for you to ask for one of the Physicians to come down from London.'

'I have every confidence in your ability,' the Earl replied. 'It is just that you are taking a devil of a time to get me well.'

Dr. Mortimer laughed.

'Like all young men, you are too impatient and always think there is something better round the corner than you are experiencing at the moment.'

He paused before he added:

'Personally, with two such lovely young ladies as Miss Mariota and Miss Lynne to look after you, I should in your place be an extremely happy man.'

The Earl for a moment looked cross, as if he resented Dr. Mortimer being so personal in his remarks. Then as if he could not help it he laughed.

'All right, Mortimer, you win! I will take it easy for another day or so, but after that I intend to rise with or without your permission.'

'So be it!' Dr. Mortimer said. 'And may I thank you, My Lord, before I leave for the case of what looked to me the most excellent wine which your servants put into my carriage when I arrived.'

'I hope you will enjoy it, Doctor.'

'That is one thing about which there is no doubt!' Dr. Mortimer replied.

When he was alone the Earl thought with a feeling of gratification that Hicks had placed quite a number of cases of wine in the cellar without Mariota being aware of it.

When he had asked his host to join him after dinner to drink a very excellent port that his sister had brought for him from the Duke's cellar, Lord Fordcombe had not disguised his appreciation.

It was easy after that to suggest that if he was drinking claret, he would feel embarrassed if the same wine was not being served downstairs in the Dining-Room.

Although he thought Mariota wished to protest, when she saw how delighted her father was with at first the claret, then the port or brandy that was offered afterwards, she could not bear to spoil his pleasure.

Because she had the feeling that whatever she said the Earl would have his own way, she accepted the food which also came with Lady Coddington and as Hicks usually hurried it into the kitchen, she pretended even to herself that she did not know how much there was.

On the Earl's instructions, Hicks not only waited on his master but also in the Dining-Room after his tray had been carried upstairs.

Mariota knew her father enjoyed the luxury of having a man-servant offer the dishes, and pour out the wine, while his daughters could sit through the meal without continually jumping up and down to fetch from the kitchen.

Because he had another man to talk to, her father spent less time in his Study, and Mariota was sure he looked forward to Lady Coddington's visits because she was so interested in the house, and also in the history he was writing.

Then she remembered that hidden away in a drawer in Jeremy's bedroom was the pretty black embroidered bag which he had stolen from Lady Coddington, and was exceedingly uncomfortable.

She told herself that only by making the Earl and his sister feel at home could she somehow erase a little of her guilt.

When dinner was finished Lynne without asking her went up the stairs, and Mariota knew she was going to see the Earl.

'You are not to talk to him for too long,' she said warningly. 'He had a headache today, and Dr. Mortimer says he must rest and sleep as much as possible.'

'You have said that before,' Lynne replied, 'but you cannot be so selfish, Mariota, as to want to keep such an attractive man all to yourself.'

'I am not trying to do that.'

'Of course you are!' Lynne argued. 'You are behaving

like an old goose with only one chick. I am not going to take him from you, I just want to talk to him.'

As she finished speaking she looked back and saw the expression on her sister's face and said quickly:

'I am sorry, Mariota. I was only teasing, dearest, and if you want to know, I feel quite certain he has fallen in love with you.'

'What do you . . mean?' Mariota asked in a voice that did not seem like her own.

'It is all the little things he says, and, dearest, if he does ask you to marry him, think how wonderful it would be for all of us!'

'I think you are crazy!' Mariota said as they reached the top of the stairs. 'How can you imagine for one moment that the Earl . . who is so important . . so grand . . would look at me?'

She gave a little laugh that was actually pathetic.

'Have you any idea what I look like compared to his sister in this gown I have worn for three years, and which is now too tight for me? And it is difficult after so many washes to know what its colour was in the first place.'

'Yes, I know, dearest,' Lynne said, 'but you are very lovely. Papa thinks so too.'

'How do you know that?' Mariota asked.

'I asked him one day if he did not think I was pretty, and he replied: "Very! And I am a good judge! But as Mariota is like your mother, you will never be as beautiful as she is." '

Mariota looked at her sister in astonishment.

'Did Papa really say that?'

'I promise you he did, and so, Mariota dear, make a little effort to make the Earl feel the same, or if you are not careful I shall try to marry him myself!'

As Lynne made the last remark with her eyes twinkling she ran ahead of Mariota and whisked into the Earl's bedroom before her sister could catch up with her.

But Mariota was not trying to. She was standing still in the passage thinking for the first time that the Earl was actually part of her fairy-story.

And her heart told her it was a very big part.

CHAPTER FOUR

'I suppose,' Lynne said as she helped herself to another piece of peach-fed ham, 'that when the Earl leaves we shall go back to rabbit, rabbit and rabbit!'

Mariota did not answer, and Lord Fordcombe was also engrossed in his thoughts.

'It will be very dull,' Lynne went on, 'and as soon as I am old enough I am going to find a man for myself who looks exactly like him.'

'In the meantime,' Mariota said with a slight edge to her voice, 'if you do not hurry with your breakfast, you will keep the carriage waiting, and you know that annoys the Squire.'

'He has not a horse in his stable as good as the one which belongs to the Earl,' Lynne said, 'so yesterday I asked His Lordship if I could ride one of his horses, and he is having one sent here for me at the week-end.'

'Lynne!' Mariota exclaimed. 'I have told you before, you are not to ask the Earl for presents of any sort.'

'He is only *lending* me a horse,' Lynne replied. 'You can hardly call that a present.'

'I am determined we will not impose ourselves on him.'

'Well, if you ask me, he has imposed himself on us,' Lynne argued. 'And if anybody deserves a present, it is Papa because it is his house and the Earl is causing a great deal of commotion by staying here.'

Lynne spoke defiantly, but she looked so lovely as she did so that Mariota knew it would be difficult for anybody to be angry with her for long.

At the same time, she thought again that the Earl had

disrupted their quiet life, and it was a mistake from Lynne's point of view.

As if he was suddenly aware what his daughters were discussing, Lord Fordcombe came out of his reverie to ask:

'How is His Lordship this morning? I was a little worried about him yesterday.'

'He had one of his bad heads, Papa,' Mariota replied, 'because he would get up when the Doctor had advised him against it. So after he had sat at the window for an hour he was quite happy to crawl back to bed.'

'Good!' Lynne exclaimed. 'That means he will not be leaving for sometime. I heard Dr. Dawson say that it was fatal for people who have suffered from severe concussion to rush about too soon.'

Mariota knew this was true, and she also felt glad, although she was ashamed to admit it, that the Earl would not be well enough to leave as quickly as he had expected to.

'The Doctor will be here soon, Papa,' she said. 'He told me he would make this one of his first calls.'

Her father quickly looked at his watch.

'I shall not wait about for him, Mariota,' he replied. 'If he wants to see me, he can come to the Study but, as you know, I am busy.'

'Yes, of course, Papa.'

Lynne finished her last mouthful of ham, then said regretfully:

'I suppose I had better go. I would like to eat a peach, but I am sure the carriage is outside.'

'I am sure it is,' Mariota agreed, 'and you can have a peach tonight, when you get back.'

Lynne rose from the table, then impulsively she flung her arms around her sister's neck.

'I am sorry if I was disagreeable, dearest,' she said. 'You are so wonderful in all you do for us, and sometimes I am a pig to you!'

'I understand,' Mariota smiled, 'and hurry, or perhaps the Squire will refuse to send the carriage for you in future, and you will have to ride to the Grange very, very slowly on Firefly.'

'I would rather walk,' Lynne exclaimed, 'it would be far quicker!'

She ran from the room as she spoke, and Mariota knew she would pick up her bonnet from the hall and be tying it on her golden hair as she ran out of the house and down the steps.

'Lynne has been lucky,' she told herself. 'Elaine Fellows likes her and the Squire has been kind enough to let them do lessons together. If we had to pay for Lynne's education I cannot think where the money would come from!'

She had the uncomfortable feeling that if there were no Governesses for Lynne, she would have to teach her, and so would her father, and she knew how much he would resent having to give up the time from his book.

All the same, he had seemed quite eager to lay it aside when Lady Coddington came, and she thought a little wistfully, that since the Earl's arrival her father had not consulted her as he usually did, or shown her what he had written.

Then she told herself that as soon as they were back to normality her father would need her as everybody else did. At the same time, things would never be exactly the same again.

She cleared the breakfast things and carried them into the kitchen for Mrs. Brindle to wash up.

Then she hurriedly went to the Drawing Room to dust it, take away the flowers that were beginning to droop, and to know, however many other things there were to do, she would have to go into the garden and pick some more.

'I hate a room without flowers,' her mother had said once. 'It looks unloved and to me flowers always mean love.'

'I suppose that is true, Mama,' Mariota agreed. 'We give flowers to people when they are happy, like when they get married, and flowers to remember them when they are dead.'

'There are far too many flowers at Funerals,' Lady Fordcombe had replied. 'I have always believed that we should give flowers to people when they are alive to show we

71

love them, and when they are dead I am sure they have enough flowers in Heaven.'

Mariota had laughed.

'That is a lovely idea, Mama, but think how upset everybody in the village would be if our wreath was not on top of the coffin.'

Now, she thought, she must pick flowers not only for the Drawing Room but also for the Earl's bedroom.

She knew it might not be possible for him to come downstairs today, and the flowers would cheer him up. So she decided to arrange several vases to make the King's Room look beautiful and smell fragrant.

It struck her that in his own house, and certainly when he was staying with the Duke, there would be huge vases of flowers from the greenhouses, perhaps orchids and malmaison carnations which her mother had told her were to be seen in all the big houses in London.

He would therefore not be impressed by the flowers in the garden outside which without being tended and cared for were almost wild.

'I suppose,' Mariota reasoned, 'that is what Lynne and I look like to him too; country girls who, although pretty, are just like weeds compared to the exotic beauties he is used to in London.'

It was almost a pain to have such thoughts. Then because she felt she wanted him to deny it was so, she ran into the garden to fill the basket her mother had always carried with every flower that was in bloom.

She arranged several vases and thought they really looked very pretty, before she went upstairs with two which she had specially prepared.

Hicks came to the Earl's bedroom door and she asked:

'How is His Lordship? May I bring these in?'

'His Lordship will be pleased to see you, Miss!' Hicks replied.

But Mariota had the idea that there was a warning note in his voice and the Earl was not in a good temper.

He was sitting up in bed, and he looked, she thought, extremely handsome, while there was no doubt that the bruise on his forehead was gradually fading from black to pale blue and brown.

She saw however there was a hard line around his lips and his blue eyes looked unusually stormy. Then he saw her, and to her surprise he smiled and she felt as if the sun had come out.

'Good morning, My Lord.'

'Good morning, Mariota. I see you have very kindly brought me some flowers.'

'I know you are unable to go into the garden today, so if Mohammed cannot go to the mountain, the mountain must come to Mohammed!'

The Earl laughed.

'I am feeling very cross.'

'I thought you would be, but Dr. Dawson will be delighted that he was right, and you were wrong.'

'I am fed up with being an invalid!'

'The old people in the village say: "You must make haste slowly," and that is what you have to do.'

'Are you preaching at me?'

'Of course,' Mariota smiled. 'Could I resist such an opportunity? I have the feeling, My Lord, you are always right, and everybody tells you so.'

'I get the message,' the Earl said. 'This is a salutory lesson for me. It will teach me not to be so sure of myself in the future.'

'I hope it won't.'

The Earl raised his eye-brows and she said:

'I think people who are leaders always have to be sure of themselves before they can make other people follow them.'

'Do you think people follow me?'

'I am sure they do.'

The way she spoke made the Earl look at her before he said:

'Have I been playing a part in one of your dream-stories, Mariota?'

Because the question surprised her, she blushed and as he watched the colour come into her cheeks he thought it was very lovely.

73

There was a little pause before he said:

'I have been dreaming too, Mariota, and I would like to see you gowned fashionably and looking like you do in my dreams.'

He spoke very softly and for a moment Mariota was almost mesmerised by what he was saying.

She could see herself in one of the high-waisted gowns that she knew were the fashion, trimmed with lace or flowers round the hem to match the puffed sleeves and the elaborate bodice.

It was of course Lynne who learnt what the fashions were from Mrs. Fellows, and brought home the *'Ladies Journal'* and other magazines for Mariota to see the type of clothes they should be wearing.

They had not the slightest chance of ever possessing such exquisite creations, but at least, Mariota consoled herself, it cost nothing to look and to dream.

Now, as if the Earl knew what she was thinking he said:

'One of the presents I intend to give to your father will be gowns for you and Lynne. So if you will give me your measurements I will send to London and order them, whether you will allow me to do so or not.'

He spoke in a manner that revealed he was aware she was going to be difficult.

She came back from her dream to reality.

'You know we could not . . accept clothes from . . you,' she said because she knew it was expected of her.

'Nonsense!' the Earl replied. 'I shall explain to your father they are part of the expression of my gratitude for being an unexpected, uninvited guest for so long, and I am sure he would not refuse my gift.'

Before Mariota could say anything he went on:

'Of course you can always throw them away, or give them to a beggar in the village.'

She laughed.

'Can you imagine anybody in the village walking about in a fashionable gown? They would be put in the stocks because everybody would think they had gone mad!'

'All the same, you must promise me you will wear the

74

gowns I intend to give you,' the Earl said firmly, 'and quite
frankly, Mariota, I do not feel well enough to have an argument about it.'

'Your head is hurting you?' she asked quickly in a
different tone.

'I shall certainly have one of my headaches if you oppose
me.'

She looked at him for a moment, her grey eyes searching
his face. Then she said:

'I have a feeling that you are not only blackmailing me,
but also getting your own way by the most underhand,
sneaky and unsportsmanlike means!'

The Earl laughed.

'Then you accept that I shall have my own way with or
without your consent!'

'I suppose so,' Mariota said. 'And it would be . . wonderful to have just . . one fashionable gown!'

'Then give me your measurements. I will give them to my
sister who will convey them to my secretary who is waiting
for his orders at Madresfield.'

'Your secretary is travelling with you?'

'I seldom go anywhere without him, and at this moment
when I need so many things, he is waiting there.'

'But surely . . he should be here . . with you?'

'I did not dare to suggest it,' the Earl replied. 'I have
already foisted myself and Hicks upon you, and as you will
not let us pay for our "board and lodging", it would be an
impossible burden to add a secretary and several grooms to
my *entourage*.'

Mariota looked embarrassed. She was aware that his
groom came over every day from Madresfield to look after
the stallion and to exercise him.

She had never thought of suggesting that he might stay at
Queen's Ford, but she thought now it was what she should
have done.

It was only because she was so ignorant of the manner in
which anybody as important and as wealthy as the Earl
would travel that it had not crossed her mind.

'I . . I am sorry,' she said after a moment.

'Forgive me,' the Earl replied. 'I was really only teasing. I am very comfortable and everything is perfect as it is.'

'I am afraid that is not true,' Mariota said unhappily. 'I am very ignorant of the way you and your friends live, but I know that the Duke is very grand and everybody talks about the parties he gives at Madresfield.'

There was a wistful note in Mariota's voice which the Earl did not miss and he said:

'As soon as I am well enough you shall have a party, but not at Madresfield.'

'No, definitely not at Madresfield.'

'Why not?'

'Papa would not let me accept the invitation, even if I received one from the Duke, because it would be impossible for us to entertain him in return,' Mariota explained. 'But why should you not want me to go there?'

She thought the Earl would have some easy explanation, but to her surprise he looked away from her with a frown between his eyes.

Because he had obviously no intention of answering her question he said:

'Have the newspapers come? I want you to read to me about what is happening in Parliament, for I think it is a mistake for me to tire my eyes after the way they ached yesterday.'

'Yes, of course I will read to you,' Mariota said eagerly.

One of the delights of having the Earl in the house was that Hicks had ordered every daily newspaper and also a number of sporting magazines which he said the Earl always read.

While he was having his headaches Dr. Dawson had forbidden him to read, and Mariota had read to him aloud everything he had asked her to.

She had also gone on reading the newspapers while he slept, and found an answer to so many things she wanted to know, besides being fascinated by what was happening in the world outside Queen's Ford.

Lynne had found the Sporting Magazines boring and begged Hicks when Mariota was not listening, to purchase some of the Ladies Magazines for them.

Mariota had been angry when they arrived, but when Hicks had explained that the Earl always bought them at his house in the country when he had lady guests staying there she had not made him cancel the order as Lynne had feared she might.

She could not bear to spend any of the precious sovereigns that Jeremy had left her on anything so frivolous.

'When the Earl leaves we shall need every penny for food,' she thought.

She knew without Lynne telling her that it was going to be very difficult to revert suddenly from the delicious, exotic dishes that were sent from Madresfield to their staple diet of rabbit.

Now she went from the Earl's room to run downstairs and see if the newspapers had arrived, only to find that Hicks had already brought them up and they were lying on a chair outside the bedroom door.

She carried them back into the room to put them down on the bed in front of the Earl.

There was *'The Times'* and the *'Morning Post'* which she knew were two newspapers he read every day, besides a number of miscellaneous others which he told her were important because they told what the opposition was thinking.

'Are these the opposition?' Mariota asked looking at the newspapers called *'The Political Register'*, *'The Courier'* and *'The Weekly Reformer'*.

'With all these newspapers here it will be very exciting for me to read them all.'

'Few women enjoy Politics.'

'Then I must be the exception,' Mariota replied. 'Whenever I get the chance I look to see what Mr. Wilberforce has said about the scandal of the climbing boys, and the horrifying reports about the employment of children in the mines.'

She looked at him a little shyly as she said:

'You are going to support those Bills when they come before the Lords?'

'Is it something you want me to do?'

'Please . . you must see how . . cruel such . . things are . . and how . . wrong.'

'Wrong?' the Earl questioned.

Then he said, and she thought cynically:

'I suppose you think it is wrong for some people to have money, and some none, and are applying it to yourself personally.'

'That is untrue!' Mariota answered quickly. 'I was not thinking of myself. There are many people far worse off than we are, even though we do find it a struggle.'

'I can understand that,' the Earl said, and now his voice was sympathetic. 'But the person who has to do the struggling, Mariota, is you!'

'I have to . . you do see I have to,' Mariota replied as if she must excuse herself. 'Papa is immersed in his book, and I have to think of . . Lynne and Jeremy, and I worry about what will . . happen to them in the . . future.'

As she spoke she thought that although Jeremy had promised her that never again would he play at being a Highwayman, when he returned from London with his new clothes he would still be bored and frustrated.

Somehow she had to prevent him from doing something else that might lead him into trouble.

The Earl's blue eyes were on her face. Then he said:

'Suppose you tell me what worries you, and let me see if I can help?'

'No . . no . . of course . . not. What you have to worry about at the moment is getting well . . and other people's troubles are always . . tiresome.'

'I would not find yours tiresome.'

He sounded so sincere in the way he spoke that Mariota looked at him in surprise, then found it very difficult to look away.

For a moment there was only the Earl's dark blue eyes and she felt as if they drew her towards him and she was lost in them.

Then because it gave her a strange feeling in her heart she hurriedly picked up a newspaper and asked:

'What would you like me to read to you today?'

'I do not mind very much,' the Earl replied. 'I like listening to your voice. You have a very beautiful voice, Mariota. It is soft and gentle while many women have hard and brittle voices which belie their faces.'

'Mama used to read to me when I was very small,' Mariota said, 'and perhaps I have copied her.'

'You are being very modest, when actually you are a very positive person,' the Earl said, 'and you have a personality which is all your own.'

Mariota looked startled.

'I have never thought of myself like that. Perhaps because Lynne is so beautiful I feel when we are together that nobody wants to look at me. And when you meet Jeremy, you will know that he is very positive, in fact, too much so.'

'I am looking forward to meeting him,' the Earl said. 'What is he doing in London?'

'He is . . with some . . friends,' Mariota said after a little hesitation.

It was only then that she thought with horror that if Jeremy returned before the Earl had left it was going to be difficult to explain where the money had come from to buy his new clothes.

'We shall have to . . invent a . . friend who has been . . kind to him,' she told herself.

Then she felt embarrassed and ashamed that once again they had to lie.

'One lie leads to another,' she remembered her mother saying once and in this case it was true.

'Tell me how I can help you,' the Earl said as if he could read her thoughts. 'Why do you not trust me, Mariota? I feel very hurt that you should shut me out of your thoughts and feelings.'

'They . . would not . . interest you . . My Lord.'

'Try me and see.'

She gave a little sigh.

'I would like to,' she answered. 'I would like to . . very much, but it is . . impossible.'

'Now you are challenging me,' the Earl said with a faint smile, 'and let me tell you, Mariota, I can never resist a challenge!'

Because he was so strong and overwhelming, Mariota gave a little cry.

'No, please . . please do not try to read my thoughts or . . find out what they are,' she said. 'They are mine . . and you are . . frightening me!'

'I think,' the Earl said very quietly, 'as you are aware I can read them and can also sense your feelings, we are close to each other in an unusual way. It is something that does not happen very often when two people meet by chance, as we have.'

Because the way he was speaking was something she had not expected, Mariota looked at him and once again she felt as if his eyes filled the whole world.

Then almost as if she was afraid he might hypnotise her into telling him what he wanted to know, she said quickly:

'Forgive me, I am almost sure I heard . . wheels outside the front door. It may be your . . sister.'

She did not wait for the Earl to answer, but hurried from the bedroom.

When she vanished the Earl lay back against his pillows staring with unseeing eyes across the room.

Although what Mariota had said had been simply an excuse to leave him because she was afraid, she thought her instinct must have told her there was actually a carriage driving up to the front door.

She went down the stairs and by the time she had reached the bottom of them there were two ladies standing in the hall.

One of them was Lady Coddington and the other was a young girl who seemed to be about the same age as herself.

She was so beautifully dressed that for a moment Mariota could only look at her pale pink gown trimmed with silk flowers, and her high-brimmed bonnet encircled by a wreath of roses.

'Good-morning, Mariota!' Lady Coddington said. 'How are you, dear?'

Mariota curtsied and replied:

'Good-morning, My Lady. I know you will be glad to hear His Lordship is better this morning.'

'I was so worried when he had such a bad day yesterday,' Lady Coddington said. 'Let me present you to Lady Elizabeth Field. This, Elizabeth, is Mariota Forde, who has been so kind to my brother that I can never be sufficiently grateful.'

'Lady Coddington has told me how wonderful you have been,' Lady Elizabeth said. 'Is His Lordship really better?'

'Better than he was yesterday,' Mariota replied, 'but he still has to be kept very quiet.'

'I am sure he will want to see me,' Lady Elizabeth said.

'I think, dear, we must ask Miss Forde to enquire first if it will not be too much for him,' Lady Coddington interrupted.

Mariota was just about to say she would do that when there was the sound of another carriage approaching and she glanced through the window.

'Here is the Doctor!' she exclaimed.

Then she gave a little cry, because Jeremy was with him.

She was so pleased to see her brother that regardless of whether Lady Coddington might think it rude, she ran through the front door and down the steps to greet him.

'I found your brother stepping from the Stage Coach at the cross-roads,' she heard the Doctor say as she flung her arms around Jeremy's neck.

'You are home! How wonderful! I have been thinking about you so much!'

'And I of you,' Jeremy replied, 'and I felt I could not stay away any longer.'

It was then that Mariota was able to step back and look at him and give an exclamation of surprise.

He certainly looked very different from when he had left.

He wore a cut-away coat that fitted without a wrinkle and was in the very latest fashion. His champagne-coloured pantaloons accentuated his slim hips, and his long legs ended in a pair of Hessian boots which shone in the sunshine.

The points of his collar reached high above his chin and his cravat, far more elaborate than she had ever seen before, was tied in an intricate style which she was sure must have taken him hours to perfect.

On Jeremy's head at a raffish angle he had a new top-hat of the same style that the Earl had been wearing when he had been flung from his horse.

'You look wonderful!' Mariota cried.

Jeremy's eyes twinkled.

'I rather thought that myself.'

'You must come and tell Papa you are back,' she began then remembered who was in the hall.

'Lady Coddington is here,' she said and there was a definite warning in her low voice. 'She was on her way to Madresfield to stay with the Duke when her brother had an accident by the roadside.'

She saw from the expression in Jeremy's eyes that he understood what she was saying.

Yet as they walked up the steps behind the Doctor she thought he was quite unabashed and very sure of himself.

'Good-morning, My Lady,' Dr. Dawson was saying.

'Good-morning, Dr. Dawson,' Lady Coddington replied. 'Elizabeth, may I introduce Dr. Dawson, who has been looking after my brother since his accident.'

'I am delighted to meet you,' Lady Elizabeth replied in a voice that sounded musical.

Even as she shook hands with Dr. Dawson she saw Jeremy behind him, and her eyes widened with surprise.

Hurriedly, because she was nervous, Mariota said to Lady Coddington:

'May I present my brother, Jeremy, who has just returned from London.'

'He will certainly be surprised to find his home invaded by a lot of strangers!' Lady Coddington remarked.

'Dr. Dawson has been telling me about his patient,' Jeremy answered.

'Let me introduce you to somebody who has come here for the first time,' Lady Coddington said. 'Mr. Jeremy Forde — Lady Elizabeth Field.'

'I have seen you out hunting,' Jeremy said, 'and I thought you rode magnificently!'

'I am sure I have never seen you, or I should have remembered,' Lady Elizabeth answered.

'I was not riding,' he replied. 'The horses we possess are only just capable of walking from one end of the drive to the other. No, I was on foot, and envying as well as admiring you.'

Lady Elizabeth laughed.

'I am very flattered, and what a pity there is no hunting now, or you could certainly borrow one of the Earl's superlative horses while he is *hors de combat*.'

'That is something I would certainly like to do,' Jeremy said.

Mariota looked at Lady Coddington.

'Shall we go upstairs,' she asked, 'and see if His Lordship feels strong enough to have an extra visitor?'

'Yes, of course,' Lady Coddington replied. 'I am sure Mr. Forde will look after Lady Elizabeth until we know the verdict.'

'It is something I am delighted to do,' Jeremy affirmed, and Mariota thought with a little smile that London had certainly improved his manners.

Lady Coddington was looking very attractive in one of her mauve gowns as she walked slowly up the stairs.

When they were out of earshot of the two people down below she said:

'Lady Elizabeth insisted on coming with me, but if the Doctor thinks it is a mistake, she will quite understand that my brother cannot see her.'

'I am sure he will want to do so,' Mariota replied.

She thought as she spoke that it would be difficult for any man not to think that Lady Elizabeth was very attractive and so exquisitely dressed that it was a pleasure to look at her.

She was not exactly beautiful, but she had a very pretty face with a dimple on either side of her mouth which showed when she smiled.

As they reached the top of the staircase she looked back

and saw Jeremy was taking Lady Elizabeth into the Drawing-Room, and she felt sure it had never crossed Lady Coddington's mind that she had seen him before.

Nevertheless as she shook hands with him Mariota had felt for a moment as if her heart had stopped beating, and her voice was constricted in her throat.

She knew how terrifying it would be if Lady Coddington had cried out that here was the Highwayman who had stolen her money.

But the expression on Lady Coddington's sweet face had not altered and Mariota felt now as if she had walked a tight-rope and by a miracle had reached the other end of it.

They arrived outside the Earl's bedroom and as they did so they could hear Dr. Dawson's voice from behind the closed door, so they stood waiting outside in the corridor.

Lady Coddington looked to where at the end of it there was a diamond-paned window letting in the sunshine which made a pattern of gold on the threadbare carpet.

'This house is so lovely!' she said almost as if she spoke to herself. 'Do you not sometimes imagine what it must have been like when it was first built, and later when your father tells me it was redecorated and refurnished after the Restoration when the King himself came to stay?'

'That is how I would like to see it now,' Mariota said, 'but it is something that will never happen.'

'I suppose not,' Lady Coddington sighed, 'but it is sad to think of all those beautiful rooms closed and the rain coming in through the roof.'

She spoke as if she really cared, and Mariota said:

'Papa minds terribly that what is so much a part of history is crumbling about his ears, but because you have been so sympathetic he has seemed much happier than he usually is.'

'Thank you for telling me that,' Lady Coddington answered. 'I have taken up so much of your father's precious time, and I hate to impose on him.'

'Please do not reproach yourself,' Mariota pleaded. 'It is very good for him to be taken out of himself, so please Lady

Coddington, while your brother is here, do spend as much time as you can spare with Papa.'

Lady Coddington smiled and put her hand on Mariota's shoulder.

'Thank you, my dear, for saying that,' she said, 'and I do hope that your father's book will be a huge success.'

'I think it very unlikely,' Mariota answered, 'but we must not tell him so.'

'No, of course not,' Lady Coddington agreed. 'That would be unkind.'

Dr. Dawson came out from the bedroom and both Lady Coddington and Mariota looked at him questioningly.

The Doctor shut the door behind him.

'A rather penitent patient,' he said with a faint smile. 'His Lordship to my surprise has admitted that yesterday was a mistake, and it is something which must not happen again. So he must be completely quiet today, and he has promised that he will try to sleep after luncheon. It is up to you, Miss Mariota, to see that he obeys me.'

'I will certainly try,' Mariota answered, 'but as he has told me often enough, he always gets his own way.'

Lady Coddington gave a quiet little laugh.

'That is true. I am afraid my brother has been spoilt ever since he was a child, and it is so much easier to give in to him than to fight a losing battle trying to persuade him to do something else.'

'That I can believe,' Dr. Dawson said, 'and My Lady, will you just stay with him for a few minutes, then come again tomorrow when I am hoping he will be back on the road to recovery.'

'Yes, of course,' Lady Coddington said. 'I will do anything you ask, and thank you for making him behave sensibly.'

She smiled at both the Doctor and Mariota, and went into the bedroom while Mariota escorted the Doctor down the stairs.

'I hope Lady Elizabeth will not be angry with me,' he said, 'but it would be a great mistake for the Earl to talk too much at the moment, even with anybody as attractive and charming.'

'You have met her before?' Mariota enquired curiously.

'I do not attend His Grace professionally,' Dr. Dawson replied, 'but I have often seen Lady Elizabeth in the distance and admired her. It seems unnecessary when she is so attractive to be also very rich.'

Mariota looked surprised because although she supposed the Duke of Madresfield must be a rich man, she knew he had two sons, so it seemed unlikely that his daughter should have inherited a great deal.

The Doctor seeing that she looked puzzled said as they went down the stairs:

'You obviously do not read the local newspapers, Miss Mariota. The *"Worcester Journal"* had huge headlines about two years ago when Lady Elizabeth came into an enormous fortune from her Godmother who was an American.'

'Papa never buys the local newspapers.'

'There was a great deal of talk about it in the neighbourhood, as you can imagine,' Dr. Dawson went on, 'and Lady Elizabeth is what is popularly called a "millionairess" in her own right.'

'How lovely for her!' Mariota exclaimed.

She found herself imagining how exciting it would be if she had a Godmother who could leave her perhaps only a small fortune, enough to do up the house, make certain that Jeremy had horses to ride, and Lynne to go to London.

Then she remembered she had just recalled the three wishes that she had told the Earl she would make if a Genie appeared.

Aloud she said:

'When my Godmother died, she left me a Prayer-Book and a picture of the Holy Family fleeing out of Egypt. I still have both of them.'

Dr. Dawson gave one of his amused laughs.

'A nice thought,' he said, 'but hardly equivalent to being left a few million!'

'No, that is true,' Mariota agreed. 'If ever I have any

children, I must be careful to choose them very rich God-parents, who will remember them in their will.'

'A good idea,' Dr. Dawson said, 'but I expect you will find in life, as I have Miss Mariota, that money goes to money, and the poor always seem to manage to stay poor.'

He laughed as if he had made a good joke and stepped into his gig which a groom had been holding, although Mariota had the idea that his horse even if he had been left free, would not have strayed more than a few feet.

'Thank you for bringing Jeremy home,' she remembered to say as the Doctor started to move away.

'I could not allow him to get his smart boots dusty,' the Doctor replied, 'and I have a suspicion that his bag was a great deal heavier when he came back than when he left.'

That was undoubtedly true, as Mariota could see, because Jeremy's bag which he had taken from the gig had been left at the bottom of the steps when he had followed her into the house.

She bent down to lift it and found it too heavy for her when a groom who was the Earl's servant came to her side to say:

'Oi'll do that, Miss. Where do ye want it put?'

'Thank you,' Mariota answered. 'That is very kind of you. Would you place it in my brother's bedroom? It is exactly opposite the one in which His Lordship is sleeping.'

'Oi'll do that, Miss.'

The groom carried the heavy case up the stairs jauntily as if it weighed nothing, and Mariota thought that if all her wishes could come true, she would certainly wish for more servants and certainly one to carry luggage up and down.

She went into the house, and as she stood in the hall she could hear Jeremy's voice in the distance and guessed that he was showing Lady Elizabeth over the house.

She was quite certain he was doing so with pride, and Mariota wondered if Lady Elizabeth with all her wealth would be scornful of the walls and ceilings stained with damp and everything in the rooms threadbare.

Then she told herself she was feeling exactly what she was afraid Jeremy and Lynne would feel when the Earl left.

'I must not compare what is happening now with what will happen afterwards,' she told herself severely. 'We are lucky, very lucky to have something new to talk about, and to have known even for a short while such interesting and delightful people.'

She knew it would be impossible for her ever to forget the Earl, and since he was now a part of her dream-world, she would feel even when he had gone that he was still with her.

She walked slowly up the stairs and as she did so, saw Lady Coddington coming to meet her.

'I have stayed with Alvic for such a little time that I am sure you are pleased with me, Mariota. I think he wants you to read to him. I offered to do so because I thought you might have something else to do, but he said he preferred your voice to mine!'

'I am sure that is not true,' Mariota protested.

'I am sure it is,' Lady Coddington smiled. 'Like all brothers, Alvic is very blunt with me when he wishes to be.'

'As Jeremy is with me,' Mariota replied.

They smiled at each other and Lady Coddington said:

'I will go and see your father, then take Elizabeth home.'

'I am afraid she will be very disappointed at not being able to see the Earl.'

'There is always tomorrow,' Lady Coddington replied, 'and I expect he will soon be well enough to come to Madresfield.'

The way she spoke made Mariota feel as if a cold hand touched her heart.

She saw waiting for the Earl the grandeur, the luxury, the people who meant something in his life and who were a part of it.

'Once he goes he will never give us another thought,' she told herself.

Suddenly it was terribly important that she should not miss one second of the time she could be with him, and without intending to she began to run down the passage towards the King's Room.

Only when she reached it did she feel breathless, not only with hurrying but also with her own thoughts.

She opened the door and walked in, and as she did so the Earl said:

'Dr. Dawson said I am to be quiet. I cannot understand why you allow all these people to pester me, knowing it is bound to give me a headache.'

Mariota walked towards the bed aware as she did so that the Earl was scowling at her.

'I am sorry,' she said, 'I thought you would want to see your sister and perhaps Lady Elizabeth just for a moment.'

'I have no wish to see anybody,' the Earl said crossly. 'Read me the Editorial in *"The Times"*, then the Parliamentary Report.'

He lay back against his pillows and shut his eyes.

Feeling as if she had been reproached for something she had not done Mariota took up the newspaper and started to read.

She had only gone a little way through the Editorial when she was aware that the Earl had opened his eyes again and was watching her.

. . . .

All through luncheon Jeremy talked while Mariota and her father listened.

He had been longing to relate what had happened in London and how exciting it had been.

'I was very fortunate in finding two men I knew when I went to the tailors,' he said. 'One of them was Maynard, who you will remember, Papa. He used to live about five miles away when we were children. The other was a man who stayed with the Squire for the hunting last year, and who came to dinner. Do you remember?'

'I remember,' Mariota said.

She remembered what a struggle it had been to produce a meal that was to Jeremy's satisfaction, and which had not only cost money they could not afford, but also a great deal of imagination.

However, the meal had in fact been excellent, and old Jacob had made a great effort to put on one of the liveried coats with its silver buttons that were kept for smart occasions, then waited quite creditably if rather slowly.

'They seemed delighted to see me,' Jeremy went on, 'and advised me which clothes to buy. Then they took me off to their Club and entertained me the whole time I was in London.'

'How wonderful for you!' Mariota exclaimed thinking in that case he would not have had to spend all his precious money.

As if he was aware what she was thinking, he said:

'You are quite right. I spent very, very little, except on my clothes.'

'You certainly look very smart,' Lord Fordcombe said as if he had noticed them for the first time, 'but why did you want new clothes all of a sudden?'

'I had grown out of my others, Papa,' Jeremy answered, 'and I either had to borrow yours, or go naked.'

'Then I am very glad you bought some new ones,' his father answered. 'Tell me what you saw in London.'

Because it had obviously not occurred to him to wonder where Jeremy had got the money to expend on new clothes, Mariota sighed with relief.

Jeremy launched into a long description of the Theatres he had attended with his friends and the Dance-Halls to which they had taken him later, and the uncomfortable moment passed.

In the short time he had been away, Jeremy had certainly filled every moment of it with amusement and she wondered how long it would be before he would feel he must go back for more.

When her father returned to his Study Jeremy said:

'Lady Elizabeth is a very attractive girl. I would like to see more of her.'

'I should not waste your time,' Mariota said.

'What do you mean by that?' Jeremy enquired.

'Lady Coddington told me that she inherited a great fortune from her American Godmother,' Mariota answered, 'and I am quite certain if you pursued her to Madresfield the Duke would think you were a fortune-hunter and send you packing.'

'I was not thinking of marrying her,' Jeremy said. 'I just thought she was attractive. I would have liked to invite her to luncheon, only I did not dare. But actually she said she would ride over here this afternoon with a groom, and I was just wondering if I might borrow the Earl's stallion to ride with her.'

Mariota looked astonished and Jeremy added with a twinkle in his eye:

'I enjoyed riding him before.'

'But surely you would not ride him again without permission?' Mariota questioned, 'and I do not like to bother the Earl.'

'Why not?' Jeremy enquired.

Mariota had no answer to this, but she told him what the Earl had promised Lynne, that she should ride on Saturday when she had no lessons and he was sending a horse from Madresfield and a groom to escort her.

'If she is riding I am certainly going to!' Jeremy said.

'No, please, Jeremy, please .. you cannot do that!' Mariota exclaimed.

'If His Lordship can avail himself of what to all intents and purposes are my stables,' Jeremy said, 'I cannot believe he would grudge me a ride on his horse.'

He walked from the Dining-Room as he spoke and Mariota realised that he had made up his mind and nothing she could say would change it.

She felt embarrassed that once again they were imposing on the Earl. When she took his tea up to him at four o'clock she found that he had slept, as Dr. Dawson wished him to do, for two hours, and thought it best to say nothing.

'I feel much better,' the Earl said as she put the tray down beside him.

He looked at it and smiled.

'I see you have made me some brandy snaps,' he said. 'I have not had them since I was a child.'

'I hope I have made them right.'

'I am sure you have,' the Earl replied, 'for amongst other virtues you are an exceptional cook.'

'I enjoy cooking,' Mariota said, 'but only when I have the right ingredients.'

The Earl sent Hicks back with a message to the Duke's Chef for everything she needed to make the dishes which he liked best.

These included ingredients for a *crème brulée*, which they had not seen for a long time, and when they arrived Mariota was so delighted at having what she thought of as 'the tools of the trade' that she did not protest but soothed her conscience by thinking that as it was for the Earl she need not feel guilty about it.

She felt at the same time, that she had strayed a very long way from her first decision that as he was their guest he must be content with what they could provide, or else go without.

Now as Mariota poured out the Earl's tea for him and sat in the chair beside the bed, she said:

'I am sorry you are not well enough to see your other caller today. Lady Elizabeth is very attractive.'

'Do you think so?'

'She is very beautifully dressed.'

She thought the Earl was about to say something, then instead he said:

'Can you play the piano, Mariota?'

It was something he had never asked her before and there was quite a considerable pause before she replied:

'Y.yes . . Mama insisted that both Lynne and I should learn to play quite well, and it is something I greatly enjoy when I have the time.'

'I would like to hear you play,' he said. 'I think somehow in my mind I have always associated you with music.'

'It is strange you should say that,' Mariota answered, 'because when I am telling myself stories and when they are happening in my dreams, there is always music in the background. It is the music of the wind in the trees, the birds waking in the early morning, and sometimes the waves of the sea become a melody which I remember when I wake.'

'When I am well enough to come downstairs, that is what you shall play for me.'

'If we had a magician in the house,' Mariota said, 'he would order the piano to fly upstairs and place it in the room next door where I could play to you now and soothe you to sleep.'

'Your voice does that,' the Earl replied, 'and that is why I was sure you were musical, Mariota. Lovely voices haunt me.'

The way he spoke, Mariota thought, it was as if he was remembering a voice that had haunted him and she was sure it was that of a lovely woman.

She thought she would like to believe that when he left Queen's Ford her voice would haunt him.

But she was certain that would be impossible because there would be so many lovely women around him that he would have no reason to remember her.

The Earl's eyes were on her face.

'You look sad, Mariota. What are you thinking about?'

'I was thinking about you,' she replied truthfully.

'What were you thinking?'

There was a little pause before Mariota managed to say:

'I was . . thinking that when you are up and about and resume your normal life there will be no time for you to be haunted with so many . . friends about you.'

The way she said the word 'friends' told the Earl exactly what she was thinking.

He smiled and said:

'Once again, Mariota, you are being very modest in under-estimating yourself.'

There was a little pause before he added:

'You know that I shall be haunted by you.'

The way he spoke made Mariota look at him in astonishment. Then he said:

'I do not wish to talk about it now. Read to me, read me anything. I just want to hear your voice.'

He sounded so strange that Mariota felt a dozen questions coming to her lips, but knew it would be a mistake to utter them.

He was obviously on edge, and fearing that despite his rest his head might be hurting him she quickly picked up the newspaper and opened it at random.

Without considering Mariota began to read aloud and then realised she was reading a description of a party given by the Prince Regent at Carlton House: how the State Rooms had been decorated, fairy-lights and fountains arranged in the garden, and the guests who were received by the Regent.

As she read Mariota's imagination made her almost see the ladies in their glittering jewels and beautiful gowns escorted by gentlemen blazing with decorations.

She found herself enthralled by the descriptions of the music which was played and the supper that was served, all characteristic of the Prince's hospitality.

She felt almost as if she could hear the brilliant, witty, scintillating conversation that filled the air.

Only when she had finished did she look at the Earl and was aware that he was watching her.

'You should have been there!' she said.

'And so should you.'

Mariota laughed.

'I would certainly have been the "Goose-Girl" in the Palace of Prince Charming and very much out of place.'

'If I remember that fairy-story correctly,' the Earl said, 'the Goose-Girl's beauty stunned them all, and the Prince fell in love with her. That, Mariota, is what should happen to you.'

She laughed a little shyly.

'In my fairy-story, yes,' she said, 'but in reality I should have hidden myself in a corner or run away, and the Prince would not even have been aware that I had been present.'

'In my fairy-story,' the Earl said very quietly, 'he would not only have found you, but would have been aware you were what he had been looking for all his life!'

CHAPTER FIVE

Mariota came back from Church and put her Prayer-Book down on the hall-table before she undid the ribbons of her bonnet and threw it on a chair.

It had been a rather more boring service than usual, and she had thought the sermon would never end.

Then she knew the truth was she was longing to get back to the house to see the Earl, and everything that prevented her from doing so seemed like a gigantic obstacle in her way.

Because the living of the Church belonged to her father and he could not afford to pay a Vicar as had always been traditional, the Services were now conducted by the Reverend Theodoceus Dowty, the very old incumbent of the next village.

This meant they had only one Service on a Sunday, and everybody crowded into the small Church from the oldest inhabitant to the youngest.

It was rather pathetic, Mariota thought for the first time, that the only entertainment in the village was the Service on Sunday, when they all put on their best clothes to see each other.

She sat alone in the huge family pew in the Chancel with the Forde coat-of-arms above it.

She prayed fervently for the Earl that he might get well, and yet at the same time she could not subdue her longing to keep him at Queen's Ford for as long as possible.

Every day it seemed to her that she dreaded more and more the moment when he would say good-bye, and she would never see him again.

It was quite an effort to force her prayers away from the Earl to her family and she prayed for them as she always had: that Jeremy would not grow bored, that Lynne would somehow, by some miracle, be able to go to London and attend the Balls like any other débutante, as her friend Elaine would be able to do.

'It is unfair that we should have so little, and have to account for every penny,' Mariota told herself.

Then she felt shocked by her own ingratitude.

Who could have imagined a fortnight ago that they would have anybody as exciting and attractive as the Earl, staying in the house?

And that they would be eating the delicious food and drink which he had insisted upon providing for them all because he needed it himself.

'I really am grateful, God,' she said.

At the same time, there was that feeling in her heart that when the Earl and everything belonging to him vanished it would be like having seen a mirage and knowing it had no reality.

Now the house seemed very quiet and she wondered where Lynne and Jeremy were.

They had both refused to go to Church with her, and she thought she had better look in the Drawing-Room to tell them she was back before she went upstairs to see the Earl.

She opened the Drawing-Room door, then stood transfixed.

Standing at the far end of room with his back to the fireplace was the Earl. He was dressed and looking so smart, so magnificent and overwhelming that for a moment she almost felt as if he was a stranger.

Then with a little cry she ran towards him.

'Why did you not . . tell me you were . . going to get up?' she asked. 'Are you well . . enough? Are you quite . . sure it is not too . . much for . . you?'

Her questions fell over themselves. The Earl smiled and said:

'Good-morning, Mariota. I am glad I have been able to surprise you.'

'I am astonished! I thought you would have to stay in bed for another two or three days . . at least.'

'I refuse to be a weakling any longer and quite frankly, I feel much better than I expected to. I have been waiting for your return so that you could share a glass of champagne with me.'

'To celebrate that you have come downstairs?' Mariota asked with a smile.

'No, to celebrate that I am a man again, and you will no longer be able to bully me as you have been doing while I was in bed!'

Mariota looked at him quickly to see if he was serious, then realised he was teasing her.

She gave a little laugh as she walked towards the table on which she now saw there was her father's wine-cooler which had not been taken from the safe for many years, and in it an open bottle of champagne.

'Shall I pour you a glass?' she asked.

'That is what I am waiting for.'

She handed a glass of champagne to him, and as she gave it to him she looked up at him and suddenly for some inexplicable reason felt shy.

She told herself it was because he was right in saying that he was a man again, and that was very different from being a patient who wanted her to look after him and who some-times, when he was in pain, seemed like a little boy who needed her protection and her comfort.

The Earl raised his glass.

'To Mariota, to whom I owe so much, far more than I can put into words.'

Mariota looked at him in surprise, and he added quietly:

'I do not know of another lovely lady who would have nursed me as efficiently as you have done.'

It was not what he said but the way that he said it which made Mariota feel the colour rise in her cheeks.

Because she felt suddenly self-conscious she walked back to the table to pour a small amount of champagne into the other glass that was waiting there.

'I ought to be toasting you,' she said, 'and I think really it should be a wish that, as in the fairy-stories . . you will live . . happily ever . . after.'

She thought the Earl might laugh, but instead there was a very serious expression on his face as he said quietly:

'That is unlikely, and I will tell you why later today.'

She looked at him questioningly and he said:

'I am going to take you driving this afternoon. Dr. Dawson has agreed that I need fresh air, but he will not let me ride or walk, and so I have ordered a Phaeton to be waiting for us after luncheon.'

'That sounds wonderful!' Mariota exclaimed. 'I have always longed to drive in a really smart Phaeton as I am sure yours is.'

'I hope it will meet with your approval,' the Earl said a little dryly.

'You can be sure of that,' Mariota laughed.

It was strange the way the Earl was looking so serious, and she wondered if something had upset him, or perhaps, although he would not admit it, he was feeling weak, and his head was hurting him.

But she had no time to ask him any questions before Lynne came running into the room.

She rushed up to the Earl to say:

'I had the most marvellous, wonderful ride! Thank you, thank you! How can you be so kind as to let me ride such superb horses? The one today was even better than the one yesterday!'

'That is what I thought myself when I ordered it,' the Earl said, 'and I am glad that you enjoyed yourself.'

'It was more glorious than I can ever tell you!' Lynne said. 'May I have some champagne?'

'Only a little,' Mariota cautioned quickly.

'I will not get "foxed" if that is what you are afraid of,' Lynne said, 'except with excitement.'

She paused before she added to the Earl:

'Why can you not stay with us for always? Then we can ride your horses, drink your champagne and eat your delicious food.'

'Is that the only reason you want me?' the Earl asked.

'No, of course not,' Lynne replied. 'It is exciting to talk to you, and I can understand why all the beautiful ladies in London are at your feet.'

The Earl laughed.

'Now you are flattering me, and may I say that I have never been in the company of two more beautiful ladies than I am at the moment.'

Lynne gave a little cry of delight, and as she did so her father came into the room.

'I heard you had come down, Buckenham,' he said to the Earl. 'You must be glad to be back on your feet again.'

'I am celebrating my return to normality with a glass of champagne,' the Earl replied, 'and I hope you will join me.'

'I shall be delighted to do so,' Lord Fordcombe replied, 'if my daughters have left me any.'

Mariota looked at him quickly to see if he disapproved, but he was smiling and as he took the glass which she had filled for him, he said:

'I drink your health, Buckenham! I should also like to thank you for the interest you have brought to Queen's Ford after arriving here in a somewhat unconventional manner.'

'I understand it was on a gate,' the Earl replied, 'although I remember nothing about it.'

Because Mariota could not bear to remember it was her fault that he had been thrown from his horse in such a disastrous manner, she went from the room to see if luncheon was ready.

When they had enjoyed what had been a superlative meal and Mariota thought she could never remember one when there had been so much laughter, the Earl said:

'When you are ready, Mariota, my Phaeton will be waiting for us, and the horses having had very little exercise lately will be restless.'

'I will not keep them more than a minute or two,' Mariota said rising from the table.

As if he suddenly thought of it, Lord Fordcombe asked:

'Where is Jeremy? Why is he not here?'

'I saw him when I was going to Church, Papa, riding across the Park,' Mariota replied. 'I expect he has either forgotten the time, or has stopped at an Inn for bread and cheese.'

Because she was aware that Jeremy was riding the Earl's stallion she did not stop to hear her father's reply, but hurried from the room.

She ran upstairs to fetch a shawl to put over her thin gown just in case it should grow cool during the afternoon, and arranged her bonnet in front of the mirror.

As she did so she remembered the fashionable bonnet that Lady Elizabeth had been wearing yesterday, and thought with a touch of depression that it would not matter what she did to herself, she would never be able to look as smart or as elegant as the Duke's daughter.

Then because she was afraid of keeping the Earl waiting she hurried downstairs to find him, as she had expected, climbing slowly and carefully into the high seat of the Phaeton.

The two horses he was driving were perfectly matched and Mariota knew were as distinctive in their own way as his stallion.

As she sat down beside him she realised they were driving alone and the groom was not travelling with them in the seat behind.

It gave her an unexpected feeling of happiness she could not explain, but she knew it was what she wanted and it was exciting to have the Earl to herself.

He drove as she expected with an expertise that was unmistakable, and as they moved down the drive she said impulsively:

'This is how I always imagined you would look.'

'In one of your dreams?' the Earl enquired.

'Yes, but the real you is even better.'

The Earl smiled and turned his head to look at her. She thought no man could look more attractive, and it was not surprising that her heart turned over in a rather unaccountable manner.

'Where shall we go?' the Earl asked.

'There is a rather pretty drive where I have not been for a long while. It is across the Park and through the woods you .

100

can see in the distance. I am sure you do not wish to be on the dusty highway.'

'Certainly not!' the Earl replied.

He turned onto the grass path that Mariota indicated to him and they drove right across the Park and found the entrance to the wood, where there was a ride that took them into the very heart of it, then out at the other end onto a path across the meadowland.

They did not talk because the Earl was concentrating on his horses, and Mariota was telling herself that this was something she would remember all her life and recapture again and again in her dream-stories.

'I tell you what I would like to see,' the Earl said breaking the silence, 'and that is the place where I fell off my horse, and the stone on which I hit my head.'

Mariota drew in her breath.

'Why do you . . want to see . . that?' she asked.

'Just curiosity,' he replied. 'I do not remember in my whole life ever falling before in such an ignominious manner, and it will remind me that "pride often goes before a fall!" '

Because she could think of no good reason why he should not go there and it was not far from where they were at the moment, Mariota directed him to what was called the Worcester Road.

They drove along it until they came to the place where Jeremy had held up the carriage and the Earl had appeared on the other side of the road.

'This is . . it,' she said in a rather small voice as the Earl drew in his horses.

There was no need to point out the large boulder against which he had hit his head when he had fallen.

She stood looking at it, and remembered all too vividly how at the shot from her pistol the stallion had reared up and he had been thrown from its back onto the stone.

'It really looks rather formidable,' the Earl said. 'Perhaps I should take it home as a souvenir.'

'No . . forget . . it!' Mariota cried.

She found herself remembering how frightened she had

101

been and how when he had pointed his pistol at Jeremy's back she had thought he would kill him.

While she was hoping that he would not speak of it, suddenly from the woods behind them through which she and Jeremy had emerged, came a harsh voice saying:

'Put oop yer 'ands!'

Mariota turned her head and gave a little cry of horror.

For one split second it flashed through her mind that it might be Jeremy playing Highwayman again.

Then she saw standing on a bank which made him almost level with them in the Phaeton was a large man holding in his hand an ancient shot-gun.

He had a handkerchief covering the lower part of his face, and a battered old hat pulled down over his forehead. His dark eyes looking at them seemed menacing, and she could see the finger of one of his huge dirty hands with its broken nails on the trigger.

'Give Oi yer money!' the man said through the handkerchief that was covering his mouth, 'or Oi'll blow a piece o' lead thro' yer!'

The way he spoke was so menacing that without thinking Mariota moved forward on the seat and stretched out her arm in front of the Earl so that he was behind her.

'You will do nothing of the sort,' she said angrily. 'This gentleman has not been well and you must not hurt him.'

'That's not me business,' the man said. 'Give Oi yer money, or it'll be th' worse for yer.'

Instinctively Mariota was aware that the Earl was thinking of what he could do to prevent them from being hurt, and at the same time strongly resented handing over his money in such an ignominious manner.

Then to his surprise, Mariota said in a different tone of voice:

'I know who you are! You are Bert Hewings! How can you behave in such a horrible manner?'

'Oi'm not arguin' wi' yer, Miss Mariota,' the man said in a surly tone.

Mariota dropped her arm which she had held in front of the Earl.

'You are crazy, Bert!' she said. 'You will be caught and hanged as you well know.'

'Might as well be 'anged as starve to death!' Bert retorted.

'Nonsense!' Mariota replied. 'And if you were to hang you know it would break your mother's heart.'

'It's no use, Miss Mariota. Oi've got t' get some money,' Bert said. 'Oi ain't 'ad a decent meal for days. Oi'm 'ungry an' that's Gawd's truth!'

'I know it is difficult to find work around here,' Mariota said quietly, 'but I will tell you what I will do, Bert. I will send a note to the Squire and see if he will find you something to do, perhaps as a woodman, or working on the farm.'

'Oi'd do anythin', Miss Mariota, yer knows that,' Bert said hopefully.

He had pulled the handkerchief from his face as he was talking, and the Earl could now see that although he was dirty and unshaven, he was not a bad-looking youth.

'I will try to help you,' Mariota said, 'but how could you think of anything so wrong and wicked as to become a Highwayman?'

'Oi hears that someun as 'eld up a carriage 'ere last week, picked oop a fortune!' Bert replied.

'Who said that?' Mariota enquired.

'Them was a' talkin' in "*The Green Man*," ' Bert answered.

This was the local Inn and Mariota realised that when the Earl's servants were searching for him they would naturally have related what had happened to them, and how they had been held up by two Highwaymen and Lady Coddington robbed.

She drew in a deep breath. Then she said:

'You must forget it, Bert, and while one Highwayman gets away uncaught, you might be hanged or transported.'

'If you take my advice,' the Earl said, speaking for the first time, 'you will hide that gun and forget that you ever carried anything so incriminating. In the meantime, here is something with which to buy food, until Miss Mariota gets you the job she has promised to find you.'

A coin spun through the air and Bert caught it deftly.

'Thank ye, Sir, thank ye!' he said, 'and Oi'll do as yer say.'

'Do not forget, Bert,' Mariota answered, 'and I promise you I will write to the Squire.'

Bert touched his hat and the Earl drove on.

As he did so Mariota thought miserably that it was all Jeremy's and her fault.

Of course the story of their ill-gotten spoils would incite the younger villagers who could not find work to try the same thing.

If it had not been the Earl whom Bert had held up, he might now have been shot by a passenger who was quicker and more experienced with firearms than he was.

They drove on for a little way before the Earl said quietly:

'Thank you, Mariota. I realise you tried to save me, and it is difficult for me to understand how you could do anything so brave as to place yourself between me and the man who was threatening us.'

'It was only poor old Bert, who is very stupid and a failure at everything he undertakes,' Mariota answered.

'I do not think you knew that at first,' the Earl said perceptively.

'No, but I could not have him shooting at you, as he might have done.'

'Why not?'

She could think of a number of answers she could give him, including that it was her fault he was here anyway. Then suddenly she knew the real reason why she had behaved as she had was because she loved him.

It was something, she thought now, that she had known for a long time, in fact from the first moment she had seen him lying against the stone on which he had struck his head, and thought how overwhelmingly smart and elegant he looked.

Then being with him, talking to him, looking after him had taken him not only into her dreams but into her heart.

She loved him, and the wonder of it swept through her like the brilliance of sunshine.

They drove on and now the Earl turned back into the

wood through which they had just come, and they moved along the ride until they reached the Park.

Then in the shadow of the trees he drew in his horses and turned round in his seat to face her.

Because she felt shy at meeting his eyes and was also still bewildered by her own feelings she asked before he could speak:

'Why . . are you . . stopping? I feel you . . should not be out for too long.'

'We will return home in a moment,' the Earl replied, 'but first, there is something I want to tell you, Mariota.'

There was a note in his voice she had not heard before and as she looked up at him her eyes met his and once again they seemed to fill the whole world.

'You are not only the most beautiful woman I have ever seen in my life,' the Earl said in a deep voice, 'but also the bravest.'

Because it was not what she had expected him to say Mariota could only draw in her breath and feel that the sunshine had a brilliance that illuminated the Earl until it glowed around him as an aura of gold.

'You must know by this time that I love you, Mariota!' he went on still very quietly with a note in his voice that seemed to vibrate through her.

'Y.you . . love me?'

She was not certain whether she whispered the words or if they were just repeated in her heart.

She felt as if everything around them exploded like fireworks which flamed up into the sky and became stars.

'Yes, I love you!' the Earl said. 'But there is nothing, my darling, that I can do about it.'

Mariota made a little gesture as if she would hold out her hands towards him, then they fell back into her lap.

'I . . do not . . understand.'

'That is what I have brought you here to tell you,' the Earl said. 'I somehow thought it would be easier than if we were in the house where we might be interrupted.'

'But you . . did say that you . . loved me?'

'Yes, I love you,' he said harshly, 'in a way I never believed was possible!'

'And . . I love . . you!'

As she spoke she saw an expression of pain in the Earl's eyes that was so poignant, so agonising that she gave a little gasp.

'What is . . wrong? Tell me . . please . . what is . . wrong?' she pleaded.

'That is what I am trying to do,' he said, 'and God knows it is the most difficult thing I have ever done in my whole life.'

Mariota clenched her fingers together in her lap and looking away from her he said, almost as if he was pronouncing his own death sentence:

'When I fell against that stone at which we have just been looking and was carried on a gate to Queen's Ford, I was on my way to stay with the Duke of Madresfield because my engagement was to be announced to his daughter Elizabeth!'

Mariota drew in her breath, then felt it was impossible for her ever to breathe again.

Then she knew she had in fact been very stupid. She should have guessed when she saw Lady Elizabeth when she came to Queen's Ford, and the Earl was too ill to see her, that there was something between them.

Because he was sitting silent, staring ahead over the Park, although she was certain he could not see the trees or the houses in the distance, Mariota said:

'You . . you are . . going to . . marry her?'

'That is what I have arranged to do,' the Earl said. 'It seemed a sensible idea, until I met you.'

Mariota gave a little quiver as he went on:

'How could I have known, how could I have guessed that there was somebody like you in the world? But I have found you too late. I had always sworn I would never marry until I was much older. But I broke my own resolution and agreed to marry Elizabeth.'

'Did you . . do you . . love her?'

Mariota could not help asking the question. It seemed to be the only thing of importance.

'I love you!' the Earl said. 'I love you with all my heart!

You are everything that I long for and want in a woman, everything I thought was quite unobtainable and no more than the foolish dreams of the boy I was many, many years ago, before I became bored and cynical.'

'But . . you do . . love me?'

'I love everything about you,' the Earl replied. 'I love your voice, your face, your big, worried eyes, and your character which is quite different from that of any other woman I have ever known.'

He made a little sound that was half a groan before he asked:

'How can you be so beautiful, and at the same time so unconscious of your beauty, and so utterly and completely selfless? You never think of yourself, Mariota, and that is why I want to think of you.'

'Do you . . think of . . me?'

'I think of you all the time, all day and all night,' the Earl said harshly. 'I cannot get you out of my mind or my thoughts. You haunt me, Mariota, with your voice and with the vibrations we both know we have for each other so that our instinct is something we cannot control.'

'That is . . what I feel about . . you!'

'We were made for each other,' the Earl said, 'and like a fool I have thrown away my one hope of Heaven.'

The way he spoke was so bitter that Mariota without thinking put out her hand and laid it on his arm.

'I cannot . . bear you to . . suffer,' she whispered.

'I am suffering,' he answered angrily. 'I am suffering because although I love you with my heart, my mind, and what you would doubtless call my soul, although I do not think I have one, I have to do the honourable thing and marry the woman to whom I have given my word as a gentleman.'

Without meaning to Mariota's fingers tightened on his arm and he held the reins with one hand and covered hers with the other.

Because they were not wearing gloves she felt herself tremble at his touch and knew that when he looked at her he felt the same.

'No other woman could make me feel like this,' he said, 'I

know too, my precious darling, that no other man has meant anything in your life.'

'There has been no . . other man.'

'That is what makes you so perfect, so unique, and mine!'

He took her hand in his and said:

'I must tell you what happened, although it is difficult to talk to you of anything but my love.'

'That is . . what I want to . . hear,' Mariota said, 'but I cannot . . bear to see you . . unhappy.'

'Unhappy? Of course I am unhappy! There will never be any happiness for me in the future without you.'

He suddenly put his hand up to his eyes as he said:

'Oh God, why did this have to happen at this particular moment? And yet, would I have it otherwise? In some way I cannot explain even to myself it is a wonder beyond words to know that you are in the same world as I am and that love is what long ago I believed it to be, and not just an illusion.'

'Of course it is . . not that,' Mariota said. 'You told me that I should . . wish for . . love . . and perhaps . . our wishes have come . . true.'

'So that we have both found love and lost it?' the Earl asked.

There was no answer to that and Mariota was silent as he said:

'I was absolutely convinced that I would never fall in love in the way you think of love and which the poets have eulogised since the beginning of time. But I had planned that perhaps in five or ten years time I would marry for the sake of family and produce an heir to carry on the title, and inherit the vast estates which my father left me.'

He paused for a moment before he said:

'Then not Eve, but a Duke tempted me.'

'He . . wanted you to . . marry Lady Elizabeth,' Mariota said beneath her breath.

'I expect you have heard how rich she is,' the Earl said, 'and because her father was understandably afraid of fortune-hunters, he suggested to me that as our two families are well matched as regards "blue blood" and fortunes, and we are both great land-owners, it would be a suitable alliance and one to which he would give his whole-hearted approval.'

'So you . . agreed!'

'I thought that Elizabeth was a pretty and attractive girl,' the Earl said, 'and as she seemed so eminently suitable, as the Duke had pointed out, to be my wife, there really seemed no justifiable reason for me to refuse the suggestion.'

'I can . . understand,' Mariota whispered.

'I suppose some part of me that I tried to forget told me this was not what I really wanted, that I had other ideas and ideals which I was throwing aside and selling myself for a "mess of potage".'

The sarcastic note was back in the Earl's voice and Mariota said quickly:

'No . . please . . it must not make you . . bitter. I want you to be . . happy. You are so kind . . so magnificent . . and I know in my . . heart you are . . everything that is . . good and . . noble.'

'How can you say such things?' the Earl asked, 'when unless I break every unwritten law as to how a gentleman should behave, I must marry Elizabeth while my heart is yours for the rest of my life.'

'You will . . forget . . me.'

He turned his head and his fingers tightened over hers as he said:

'Look at me, Mariota!'

She raised her eyes to his and he looked at her for a long moment before he said:

'You love me! I can see it in your eyes and feel it as your fingers tremble beneath mine. Will you forget?'

'That . . is . . different.'

'There is no difference in love,' the Earl said. 'I shall never forget you, just as you will never forget me. Yet can you imagine what I will go through wondering what is happening to you, wondering what you are feeling, and if you are as unhappy as I shall be.'

'As I have said . . I do not want to be . . unhappy.'

'How can I be happy without you?' the Earl asked. 'How do you think I shall feel when, waited on by servants, I shall think of you slaving away trying to keep your house habitable for your father, your brother and sister? Somehow I must try to make things better for you, but it will not be easy.'

'No, no . . of course not . . I could not take . . anything from . . you,' Mariota said quickly.

His fingers tightened on hers until they hurt.

'Do you really imagine,' he asked, 'that I can eat Caviar and think of you dining off rabbit, or drink champagne while you drink water? Be sensible, my sweet, and realise I shall suffer all the horrors of hell everytime I eat, sleep or ride one of my horses.'

'Those . . things are not really . . important.'

Because the Earl was touching her it was hard even to listen to what he was saying, when she could feel the strength of his fingers making her thrill to him as if he drew her by invisible cords.

She wanted to be near him, to be close to him, but she understood why he was telling her this when they were in a position that made it impossible for him to hold her closer to him.

All she could think of was that he loved her and in spite of what he was saying the sunshine was still there within her breast.

'I want to wrap you in sables and ermine,' the Earl went on. 'I want to cover you with jewels, but most of all, my darling, I want you with me by day and by night as my wife, as the woman I will worship for ever and who would one day be the mother of my children.'

His words seemed to come slowly, each one like an axe cutting down a young tree in its prime, and for the first time since he had been talking Mariota looked into the future and saw that for her it was dark and without him filled with despair.

'Are you surprised that I had headaches when I should have been getting better, when I have lain awake night after night wondering how I can extricate myself from the trap into which I have fallen?'

He paused before he added:

'If I asked you to come away with me, and go abroad until the fuss about Elizabeth was over, would you do it?'

Mariota knew he was waiting for her answer, and after a moment she said:

'I want to do . . anything you . . ask of me, but not if it would . . hurt or . . defame you. I am aware that if as you say you are . . engaged to Lady Elizabeth and you . . jilt her, her father might call you out and you would have to fight a duel. It would be like . . cheating at cards and could spoil for ever your . . image as a . . sportsman.'

The Earl gave a sigh that seemed to come from the very depths of his being.

'You understand! Oh, my precious, you understand! Could anybody be more wonderful?'

He lifted her hand and just for a moment his mouth lingered on her skin and she felt it was more passionate and demanding than if he had kissed her lips.

Then he released her and started the horses off along the path through the Park.

She knew as he did so that there was nothing more they could say to each other, nothing but a repetition of their love which because they now acknowledged it seemed to Mariota to burn with a fire which consumed her, and which she knew was burning in him.

Only as the house drew nearer did she say in a voice that trembled:

'I love you . . with all of me . . and I will go on . . loving you for the . . rest of my life!'

'You are not to say that,' the Earl said. 'One day you will find a man to look after you, and you will marry him. But I cannot bear to think of it at the moment.'

'I will never . . marry because I could never find a man who . . looked like you, and whom I could . . love as I . . love you,' Mariota said. 'So I shall be an "old maid", looking after Papa and the house . . and dreaming of you.'

'And will that be enough for you, or for me?' the Earl asked savagely.

Then because there was no answer they drove in silence until they reached the front-door.

CHAPTER SIX

All night Mariota was alternatively lifted into the clouds with elation to think that the Earl loved her, then cast into the depths of despair because she knew she must never see him again.

When they got back to the house she was aware that he was so emotionally moved by what they had said to each other that on getting down from the Phaeton he had walked straight in through the front-door, and up the stairs to his bedroom.

She deliberately lingered because she knew that for the moment she must not talk to him, must not make things worse than they were already.

She patted the horses, telling the groom how splendid they looked and how well they had behaved, then slowly, feeling as if a chapter of her life was closed, she walked into the house.

Because she thought she should see if Lynne and Jeremy were there, she went first into the Drawing-Room.

There was no sign of them and she was just about to go upstairs and take off her bonnet when Jeremy put his head round the door.

'Where have you been . . .?' she began, but he interrupted her by saying:

'That is the most magnificent Phaeton I have ever seen!'

'I know.'

'Why has the Earl brought it here?' Jeremy asked coming further into the room.

'He took me . . driving,' Mariota replied in a voice that

did not sound like her own, 'and I think . . tomorrow he will be . . leaving us.'

'Leaving?' Jeremy exclaimed.

There was a little pause. Then he said:

'Then I must certainly go and look at it now.'

'You are not to try and drive it,' Mariota warned, but he had already left the room and she had the feeling he had not heard her.

She thought as she went upstairs that Jeremy would also be upset at knowing that when the Earl left his stallion would go too.

She was aware, although he had said nothing to her, that he had been riding it morning and afternoon, and she was therefore not surprised when a little later she looked out of the window to see Jeremy disappearing through the trees in the Park on the Earl's black stallion.

'Perhaps it is the last time he will ever ride such a magnificent horse,' she thought.

She knew that when the Earl left tomorrow there would be so many 'last times' that she could not bear to think of them.

And yet they were there in her mind, and almost unconsciously she began to count them:

The 'last time' she would see him, the 'last time' she would talk to him, the 'last time' he would tell her that he loved her . . .

Finally there would be the 'last time' they would eat such delicious food or drink such fine wine, the 'last time' Jeremy would ride a horse like the Earl's stallion, and the 'last time' that Lynne would be mounted on a well bred, perfectly trained horse, as Mariota suspected she was riding at this moment.

What it all added up to for her personally was that it was the 'last time' she would ever love anybody as she loved the Earl.

She sat down on the stool in front of her dressing-table and put her hands up to her eyes.

Even as she felt the darkness of despair creeping over her she tried to think of how grateful she was for having known

113

him, and how whatever happened in the future she would have her memories!

But it was very poor comfort.

As she had expected, the Earl did not come down to dinner and she thought that apart from the fact that he was physically tired, it would be too emotional for both of them to face each other across the Dining-Room table with the family watching them.

Actually when dinner was served there was only her father and Lynne and no sign of Jeremy.

When Lord Fordcombe came into the Dining-Room he had seemed to be more absent-minded than usual and did not notice his son was not there. But Lynne asked somewhat aggressively:

'Where is Jeremy? If he is riding I think it very mean of him not to have asked me to go with him.'

'I think you have been riding quite long enough for one day,' Mariota said, 'and I went to Church alone.'

'If I had come with you,' Lynne answered sulkily, 'all I would have prayed for would have been a horse, and I doubt if they would drop me one down from Heaven.'

There was silence. Then her eyes lit up.

'Do you think the Earl would let me keep *Daffodil* while he is staying at Madresfield? The grooms told me he was ridden there by one of the outriders, and cast a shoe on the way, so he only arrived the day after the Earl was injured.'

Mariota did not say anything, but thought how fortunate it had been that when Jeremy held up the carriage which contained Lady Coddington it had been the Earl alone who had come from the wood and been prepared to kill him.

Had there been another man with him they might easily both have been dead by now.

'Jeremy must . . never take such . . risks again,' she told herself.

At the same time she knew that the money he had obtained would not last for ever.

Although he had promised that he would never risk her life for his own another time, she could not help feeling he would be thinking out something else which would seem like a prank, but might easily have disastrous consequences.

'I must talk to him,' she told herself.

Again she had the feeling that the Earl's horses and the way everything had changed since he came to Queen's Ford would have results which would ripple out as when a stone is thrown into water into infinity.

Although the food was delicious, Mariota realised at the end of dinner that she had not tasted it and might just as well have eaten sawdust.

Lynne had been quiet because she was thinking over how she could approach the Earl about *Daffodil*, and as Mariota left the table she asked:

'Can I not see the Earl now and say good-bye to him?'

'I think as he was really very tired after his first day out and has retired to bed,' Mariota replied, 'it would be selfish and unkind to bother him at the moment.'

'I expect you will see him.'

'No, I am not seeing him!' Mariota replied firmly. 'And it will be too early in the morning for you to say good-bye before you leave for the Grange.'

She saw the disappointment in Lynne's eyes and added:

'What I suggest you do is write to him a letter, thanking him for allowing you to ride his horse, and sending a groom with it. Say that you hope to see him again to thank him personally before he leaves Madresfield.'

Even as she spoke she thought this was unlikely, but it was the right thing to do, and also the Earl might understand how desperately Lynne wanted to go on riding, if only for a few more days.

'If I do that,' Lynne asked, 'will you suggest to him, Mariota, that he leaves *Daffodil* here, until he goes back to London?'

'I will try,' Mariota replied, 'but I can not really make any promises.'

'I suppose that is better than nothing!' Lynne said. 'But whether he comes back or not, we shall miss him.'

'Yes, we shall . . miss him,' Mariota agreed, but she was not certain whether she said it aloud or in her heart.

115

When she went to bed she had thought that she would cry, but instead she lay in the darkness thinking she was past tears.

All she could think of was the Earl's face when he had told her that he loved her, and the pain in his eyes which she realised now she had seen before when he looked at her as she moved about his room, or when she read to him.

She had not understood at the time what he was feeling but now, because she felt the same, she knew that in losing him she lost half of herself.

'I love him! I love him!' she thought miserably, and cried out to her mother feeling that she alone would understand.

Because she was like her there would be only one man in her life for whom she could feel what she felt for the Earl.

Just before dawn came, Mariota slept a little from sheer exhaustion, then awoke with a start to find that it was after eight o'clock and she had missed giving Lynne her breakfast and seeing her off to the Grange.

It was a very unusual thing for her to do, and yet this morning it did not seem to matter.

Instead of dressing quickly and rushing down the stairs she lay thinking that she was afraid of facing what lay ahead and having to watch the Earl drive away in his Phaeton.

For one moment she thought she could not face it. She would go and hide in the wood until he had gone, or perhaps lock herself in the unused part of the house among the dust and the cobwebs.

Then she thought it would only make it worse for him, and it suddenly seemed as if he was more like her son than the man she loved and she wanted to protect him and save him from being hurt or unhappy.

'I want him to be happy,' she said aloud.

Yet she knew that the agony of knowing he would marry Lady Elizabeth was like a thousand knives being turned in her heart and the pain was almost unbearable.

She dressed herself slowly and was nearly ready when old Jacob, wheezing from coming up the stairs, knocked on the door.

When Mariota opened it she saw that he carried in his

116

arms a huge box and as she stared at it in surprise she suddenly remembered what it contained.

'There be four o' these downstairs, Miss Mariota,' Jacob said. 'Oi'll bring 'em up for ye, if ye like, but it be a tirin' job.'

'No, leave them for the moment,' Mariota answered, 'and I will ask Mr. Jeremy to help you with them.'

'Thank ye, Miss,' Jacob said. 'Me legs ain't wot they used to be.'

It was inscribed on the outside in fulsome writing with the name of the shop from which it had come, and she knew this was the present the Earl had insisted on giving her after he had persuaded her to provide him with her measurements and Lynne's.

'A parting present,' she thought bitterly.

Then when she opened the box she gave a gasp. Inside were two gowns, and she had never thought anything could be so beautiful and so different from what she had ever worn before.

They were both in pale pastel shades which she knew became her, and because they were day-gowns it took a little time for her to decide which of them she would wear, knowing it would be unlikely that the Earl would ever see her wearing the other one.

Finally she chose the gown of very pale 'love-in-a-mist' blue which seemed to accentuate the whiteness of her skin, the silver in her hair and the depth of her grey eyes.

It was trimmed with shadow lace, and when she put it on she felt almost as if it had been fashioned by fairy fingers, and she looked like a nymph that had risen from the lake, or dropped down from the sky.

She stood in front of the mirror and she would have been very foolish if she had not realised that she looked lovelier than she had ever looked before. Also she had no idea that she had such a perfect figure.

'It is how I want him to remember me,' she thought and the pain in her heart took away the light from her eyes.

Slowly she went downstairs, and as she had expected the

Dining-Room was empty, and it was obvious that the rest of the family had eaten and gone.

The egg which was left for her was cold and unappetising, but she ate a little of the delicious ham which the Chef had sent from Madresfield and drank a cup of coffee which was also cold.

Then being careful not to spoil her new gown she cleared the breakfast things as she always did, and carried them into the kitchen.

"Ow many'll there be for luncheon, Miss?' Mrs. Brindle enquired.

'I do not know whether Mr. Jeremy will be back, but I expect so,' Mariota replied, 'and that should make it three.'

'Mr. 'icks says as 'e thinks His Lordship'll be leavin' this morning,' Mrs. Brindle remarked conversationally.

'Yes . . I expect he will,' Mariota replied.

She went from the kitchen into the Drawing-Room to dust and tidy it as she always did.

The syringa in one of the vases was dropping and she thought as she looked down at the petals scattered on the polished table that they were like tears.

Then she told herself it was foolish to think of such things, and when the Earl came to say good-bye she must control her feelings and try not to add to his unhappiness.

It was a long time later when she was wondering what was happening upstairs that the door opened and the Earl came in.

He was looking magnificent as she had expected he would, and for the moment she could only stare at him as he stood in the doorway feeling her voice had died in her throat.

Then he shut the door and came towards her saying:

'I knew you would be here.'

'I . . I was . . waiting for . . you.'

'And thinking of me?'

'How could I . . think of . . anything else?'

The words seemed unnecessary, and yet they were speaking them and all the time he was coming nearer to her.

118

When he was close she looked up into his eyes and saw not only the pain in them but the dark lines beneath them which told her he too had spent a sleepless night.

He stood looking at her for what seemed a long time. Then he said:

'Yesterday, when I told you that I loved you, I did so deliberately in the wood so that it would be impossible for me to hold you close and kiss you as I wanted to.'

He paused before he went on in a voice that seemed raw with pain:

'I thought it would make it worse for us both, but now I cannot go away without kissing you, Mariota, without pretending for one moment of time that you are mine.'

'I . . I shall . . always be . . yours.'

'Last night,' he went on, 'I went through all the temptations of hell, knowing that you were so near to me and it would be easy for me to come to your room to tell you how much I loved you.'

'Why . . did you . . not do so?'

'Because, my precious darling, I love you not only as a woman, who God meant to be mine, but I also worship you as somebody pure and sacred, and I could not do anything to spoil you.'

Mariota gave a little murmur and because the Earl's eyes held hers captive she could not speak, and it was hard to breathe.

'Good-bye, my darling, my precious one, the only woman I have ever loved,' the Earl said brokenly.

Then slowly, as if he wished to remember exactly what was happening, he put his arms around her, and drew her close against him.

Still slowly and very gently, as if he was touching a flower, his lips found hers.

To Mariota it was as if they moved to music, and it was the music she had heard in her dreams.

She felt as if she was dreaming, and as the Earl's lips touched hers she felt as if he was carrying her slowly up into the sky and the light from the sun enveloped them both with a halo of glory.

119

Everything she had longed for and dreamt about, everything which had seemed to her so beautiful that it lifted her heart and her mind, was there on his lips.

Then as his arms instinctively tightened about her, as her mouth was very soft, sweet and innocent beneath his, his kiss became more possessive, more insistent and he drew her closer and closer still.

It was so wonderful, so perfect, so much part of her prayers, that it was like touching the stars, and at the same time feeling the heat of the sun moving within her until shaft after shaft radiated out from her heart and through her lips and became part of the Earl.

As if he felt the same he kissed her passionately, then wildly, frantically, as if he was fighting against losing her, and yet knowing even as he did so that the battle was lost.

He raised his head and Mariota whispered breathlessly:

'I . . love you . . I love . . you . . how can I tell you how much I . . love you?'

As if her words excited the Earl more than he was already he pulled her closer to him again, and kissed her eyes, her cheeks, the softness of her neck, then again her lips fiercely, passionately and insistently.

It was as if a tempest raged over her, and yet she was not afraid. She only felt the sunshine within her turn to fire, and she knew it had been ignited by the fire within the Earl which was consuming them both.

This was love, a very human love, and yet because as he had said he loved her as if she was something sacred, she knew he would never hurt her.

Then as if they both broke under the strain, the Earl released her to walk to the mantelpiece and stand holding onto it, staring down into the empty fireplace.

'Forgive me,' he said in a voice that did not sound like his own. 'I did not — mean this to — happen.'

'There is . . nothing to forgive,' Mariota said. 'I love you as you . . love me . . but, oh, my darling, I do not want you to suffer.'

As she spoke she felt him draw in his breath.

Then as she looked up at him she saw the agony in his

face, and the lines that seemed to be etched so sharply that he seemed immeasurably older than he had before.

'I must leave you,' he said. 'To stay here is to torture us both. It is wrong, and yet I find it hard to say the simple words "good-bye".'

'Perhaps it is . . something we should . . not say,' Mariota faltered. 'Perhaps we should have . . faith that one day we may . . find each other again.'

Even as she spoke she knew it was a forlorn hope.

Lady Elizabeth was very young, a year younger than herself, and once the Earl was married only death could separate him from his wife.

There was silence. Then he said:

'Let me look at you, so that I can remember how you look at this moment! That is something that nobody can take from me.'

'I . . I am wearing the gown which . . you gave me.'

It was an effort for the Earl to take his eyes from hers and look down at the gown, but then he said:

'You look very lovely in it, but to me you have never looked anything else. You have always been clothed in dreams.'

'That is where we will meet . . at night,' Mariota said softly, 'I shall dream of you . . and if you will dream of me perhaps . . we shall . . feel that we are . . together.'

As if once again her words snapped the Earl's self-control he said harshly:

'I do not want you in my dreams, I want you in my arms, and your body close to mine. I want to talk to you, to listen to the music in your voice when you say you love me . . .'

'I do love you,' Mariota said, 'and because I love you I know that you will do many . . great and good . . things in the . . world.'

'But not without you,' the Earl protested. 'You know I can do nothing without you.'

He stared at her and now there was a different look in his eyes from what there had been before. Then he said:

'Dammit! Why are we crucifying ourselves in this idiotic way? Come away with me, Mariota, as I have asked you to do before. It will be a "nine days wonder", then everybody will talk about something else.'

As he spoke he put out his hand towards her and Mariota knew she only had to take one step to touch him and tell him she would do as he asked.

She thought how marvellous it would be to be alone with him, even if nobody else in the world spoke to them.

'In a year who will remember what happened today?' the Earl asked. 'Elizabeth is young, beautiful and rich. There will be plenty of men only too willing to marry her, and she is not in love with me any more that I am in love with her.'

His voice was very beguiling as he went on:

'Come with me, Mariota, come with me, my darling, and we will be in Heaven together, and close the gates so that nothing unpleasant can intrude on our happiness.'

There was silence, then Mariota said:

'You know I . . want to be with you . . you know I love you . . and just as you did not come to my . . bedroom last night . . I know that I cannot let you do something which is wrong!'

Her voice broke but she continued:

'Because you are so important . . so much admired, it would cause those who follow your lead also to do . . things that are wrong or even commit . . crimes they would not . . otherwise have thought of doing.'

She drew in her breath before she added:

'That is the responsibility of being who you are . . not only as an Earl, but as a man . . as a personality and a . . great Englishman.'

She was not choosing the words she spoke, they somehow came to her mind almost as if they were put there, but she knew as she spoke them that they were true, and neither of them could deny it.

The Earl was still. Then he said:

'If that is what you want and believe is right, my perfect one, then I must abide by it.'

There was a note of sadness in his voice and Mariota thought it even more persuasive than when he pleaded with her, but she knew that all she really wanted was to be in his arms.

She did not move and after a moment the Earl walked to the door and opened it.

Mariota waited, then she heard him say:

'Is that you, Jacob? Will you go to the stables and tell them I want my Phaeton brought round immediately.'

'Very good, M'Lord!'

Mariota heard old Jacob's feet shuffling across the floor, and the Earl came back to the Drawing-Room shutting the door behind him.

He walked to her side, put his arms around her, and drew her to the window.

She suddenly felt exhausted as if she had passed through a tornado, and she laid her head against his shoulder.

He did not speak, and they just stood there looking out into the untidy garden with the flowers and shrubs growing wildly, and beyond where the lake reflected the blue of the sky which seemed to echo the gown which Mariota was wearing.

Because the Earl's arm was around her and she was close to him, she felt as if they were one person, and their vibrations joined with each other.

She was sure too that the melody she heard in her mind was also in the Earl's.

They stood there for what seemed a very long time. Then he said:

'You will pray for me?'

'You know I . . will.'

'I shall need your prayers, for without them I may fail to do all the things you expect of me, but I promise you I shall always be thinking "This is what Mariota wants of me", "This is what she would wish me to do".'

'You will never fail . . in anything you . . undertake,' Mariota said softly.

'Only in the one thing that matters,' the Earl replied bitterly.

Again there was silence. Then as they heard footsteps outside in the hall and the door opened, they moved apart.

Old Jacob came plodding down the room.

'Oi went to th' stables, M'Lord,' he said to the Earl, 'but Yer Lordship's Phaeton ain't there and th' groom says when Yer Lordship asked for it, 'e were to send this letter into the 'ouse for Miss Mariota.'

The Earl did not speak and Mariota thought with a feeling of dismay that Jeremy must have borrowed the Phaeton and not yet returned with it.

It was the sort of prank he would play, expecting, she supposed, that the Earl would not be leaving before luncheon. Yet she thought she had told him he might go during the morning.

She took the note from Jacob's hand wondering who had written to her. Then as he slowly went from the room she said to the Earl:

'I am sorry . . very sorry . . but I am sure Jeremy . . will not be long.'

Because she felt how embarrassing it was that her brother should have imposed on the Earl in such an inconsiderate manner, she did not look at him but down at the note she held in her hand.

To her surprise she saw that it was addressed in Jeremy's hand-writing.

She thought perhaps it was to explain where he had gone and how long he would be away.

Feeling angry that he should be so inconsiderate she opened the letter quickly, and found that it contained two pages.

It began:

'Dearest Mariota,

When you receive this I shall be married, and I suppose you will have to apologise to His Lordship that I have taken his Phaeton and will be unable to return it for sometime . . .'

Mariota gave a little gasp, then read on:

'I fell in love with Elizabeth as soon as I saw her, and she with me, and thanks to the Earl's stallion we have

124

been seeing each other every available moment of the day.

When you told me yesterday that the Earl might leave this morning, I realised my only chance of preventing his engagement to Elizabeth from being announced publicly was to marry her first. I arranged everything with the Reverend Dowty who is so old and doddery that he has no idea that "Miss Mary Elizabeth Field" is the Duke's daughter, and of course as he has known me all my life, he has made no difficulties about performing the ceremony, and thinks the reason for such secrecy is that Elizabeth is in mourning.

The only lie I have told was to make her the same age as myself and the ceremony will therefore be completely legal.

However, in case the Duke or the Earl try to take Elizabeth from me and find some way of annulling our marriage, we are going to disappear until all the recriminations have blown over, and it is safe for us to come back from where we will be enjoying a blissful honeymoon.

I shall know it is safe to return when you put a message for me signed "Mariota" in the Personal Column of "The Morning Post", which I shall contrive to buy wherever we are hiding.

Dearest Mariota, do this for me, and of course do everything you can to prevent our being discovered too quickly. First of all, keep the Earl from communicating with the Duke for as long as possible. I am fetching Elizabeth very early in the morning before everybody is awake and she is leaving a note to say that she is coming over to Queen's Ford to be with the Earl on his journey back to Madresfield.

This will keep everybody from being curious until the Earl himself appears and they realise that Elizabeth is not with him. By that time I hope we will be far away, and I know you will think I have been very clever in all my plans when I told Elizabeth to pack some of her clothes in one of the Earl's trunks which were waiting for him, and to tell the footman he needed it to bring his clothes from Queen's Ford.

What was more, as I know it is a question you will ask, Elizabeth and I have enough money for our honeymoon, but I would marry her if she had not a penny. I love her for herself, she is the most wonderful girl in the world but of course it makes things easier than if we had to scrimp and starve, as you have been doing these last years. And at least I shall not have to eat rabbit!

Fortunately I did not pay my Tailor's bill when I was in London, and practically everything I "obtained" in that criminal manner of which you so disapproved is in the Bank. Implemented with the money and jewellery which Elizabeth is bringing with her we will be very comfortable.

I think I have thought of everything and, although you may be angry with me for what I am doing, I am sure you will think I have in fact, been very resourceful. You are a wonderful sister, Mariota, and Elizabeth is sure she will love you as much as I do, so please give us your good wishes for a happiness we are quite certain we are going to have together.

Do not forget to let us know when we can come back to civilisation, but there is no hurry, as we are both determined to have the most perfect honeymoon any two people have ever enjoyed together.

With love from your resourceful brother,
                                                    Jeremy.

While she was reading the letter Mariota had held her breath until she reached the end, feeling that this could not be true.

Then as she did not know what to say or what to think she merely handed the two closely written sheets of writing-paper to the Earl.

He took it from her with a look of surprise, but he did not ask any questions, and began to read what Jeremy had written, while Mariota stood looking out with blind eyes into the garden, her fingers clenched together.

She could not even wonder what he would think or what he would feel. She only felt unsure of herself and a little frightened.

It seemed to take him a very long time to read the letter, but when he had done so, he folded it up and returned it to her.

She took it from him and as her eyes searched his face, wondering what he was feeling he said:

'I have changed my mind! I shall not be leaving until this evening, and only when I am ready to go, you will show me that letter which I have not yet read.'

'I . . I do not . . understand . . you mean . . .?' Mariota stammered.

'I mean, my darling,' the Earl said with a smile which illuminated his face, 'that we must give the young couple a sporting chance to get away as far as possible before the hue and cry begins.'

Then as Mariota stared up at him wonderingly, his arms went round her and his lips came down on hers.

CHAPTER SEVEN

The Earl of Fordcombe was working at his desk when the door opened and Lady Coddington looked in.

'Forgive me for bothering you,' she said in her soft voice, 'but I cannot find anybody, and I wondered where my brother might be.'

There was a smile on Lord Fordcombe's face as he rose to his feet.

'I am so delighted to see you!' he exclaimed. 'I have finished the chapter about the part my ancestor played in Marlborough's Campaign and I want to read it to you.'

Lady Coddington came further into the Study and shut the door behind her.

'How exciting!' she said. 'I am longing to hear it.'

She walked as she spoke towards the desk, and Lord Fordcombe realised it was the first time he had seen her in anything but mourning.

Instead of the black or mauve gowns she had been wearing since she first came to Queen's Ford she had on a very attractive gown of white trimmed with ecru lace, run through with rows of sapphire blue velvet ribbons.

Her bonnet was also white except for blue ribbons to match those on her gown, and some tiny blue ostrich feathers peeping over the brim.

He looked at her for a long moment. Then he said:

'You look very lovely and almost like a young girl on the threshold of life.'

Lady Coddington looked shy. Then she said:

'I wish that was true, except that perhaps now I am older I am wiser and more — appreciative.'

Lord Fordcombe looked surprised at the last word, and she explained:

'When one is young one takes so much for granted, but when one is older one savours everything that happens, and is very, very grateful for any happiness one finds.'

'Sometimes I have thought I have forgotten how to be happy,' Lord Fordcombe said, 'but talking to you about my book has given me a new enthusiasm for it, and perhaps also for living.'

Lady Coddington drew in her breath.

He came from behind his desk and they moved as if by instinct towards the sofa which, worn and faded, was on one side of the large fireplace.

Lady Coddington sat down, then she said:

'I expected Alvic to come to Madresfield for luncheon, but I am sure that when the moment came to leave he decided he would stay here with you a little longer.'

'It has been a great pleasure to do what we could for him.'

Lord Fordcombe spoke as if he was not thinking of what he was saying, and his eyes were on Lady Coddington's face. Then he said in a different tone from the one he had used before:

'I suppose if your brother leaves us today I will not see you any more.'

There was silence. Then Lady Coddington said in a voice that had a little tremor in it:

'It will be — difficult, once I have — left Madresfield.'

'You know how much I shall miss you.'

'Are you — sure you will do — that?'

'It is difficult to put into words what a difference your company has made to me, and how when you leave the sunshine seems to go with you.'

Lady Coddington looked up at him and her fingers were clasped tightly together in her lap. Then she said in a voice a little above a whisper:

'I shall — miss — you!'

Lord Fordcombe rose to his feet and walked across the room to stand at the window.

He stood looking out as if he had never seen the garden

before or the trees in the Park, and after a moment almost as if the words were jerked from between his lips, he said:

'I have nothing to offer you!'

He did not hear Lady Coddington move, but suddenly she was beside him, and he was aware of the closeness of her and the sweet fragrance of the scent she used.

She stood very still without moving and after a moment Lord Fordcombe said:

'You know the position I am in. You have seen my house, and what has happened to my children.'

'But there is . . you.'

The words were almost unaudible.

Lord Fordcombe turned round and she thought no man could look so handsome, so attractive, and yet she was still afraid she had misunderstood what he had said.

She raised her eyes to his beseechingly, and he said in a voice that was low and hoarse:

'What can I say? I want you, I need you, I love you!'

There was no need to speak. Lady Coddington gave a little cry of sheer happiness and moved into his arms. . . . . .

. . . .

Mariota and the Earl found their way across the uncut lawn through bushes of syringa and lilac to an arbour.

'Nobody will find us here,' Mariota said, 'and you must sit down and rest. I am sure Dr. Dawson will disapprove of your doing too much or getting over-excited.'

'I am over-excited!'

The Earl pulled Mariota almost roughly against him and kissed her until they were both breathless.

'I love you,' he said, 'and now there is nothing to prevent me from saying so. We will be married as soon as it is humanly possible.'

Before Mariota could answer him he kissed her again, and only when finally she was free did she indicate a battered and torn old sofa at the back of the arbour and say:

'Please sit down . . I feel as if my . . legs will no longer . . support me.'

The Earl laughed, then seated himself a little gingerly on the sofa, and found that although it looked so dilapidated it was comparatively strong and quite comfortable.

He would have pulled Mariota down beside him, but she fetched a wooden stool and placed it in front of him so that he could lift his legs onto it, before she said:

'If your sister comes over this afternoon she will wonder what has become of us, but it would be a . . mistake for her to learn too . . quickly that Elizabeth is . . not here.'

'That is why I told you we had to hide,' the Earl said, 'and may I say it is something I am very happy to do with you, my lovely one.'

'I cannot believe what has happened is true! And now you do not have to . . marry Elizabeth are you quite . . certain that you . . want to marry me?'

'Are you really asking such an idiotic question?'

Then he looked at Mariota's face and asked:

'What is worrying you?'

'How do you . . know I am . . worried?' she parried.

'I love you,' he answered, 'and because of it I know every expression in your eyes, every inflection in your voice, and even now, when I feel as if I am jumping over the moon, I know that you are worried about something.'

He would have put his arms round her, but Mariota moved a little way from him before she said:

'I . . I have . . something to tell you . . and perhaps it is . . foolish of me to do so . . because when you hear what I have to say . . you will no longer . . love me . . or want to marry me.'

'Is this the secret worry of which I have been aware ever since I have known you?' the Earl asked.

'Y.yes!'

'Then whatever it is,' he said, 'let me make it clear that even if you had committed every crime in the calendar I would still love you, and I would still marry you. You are mine, Mariota, and nothing and nobody shall prevent us from being together for the rest of our lives.'

Mariota made a sound that was curiously like a sob before she said:

'You must . . hear what I have to . . tell you . . first.'

'I am listening.'

He knew as he spoke that she was trembling, and only because he wished to do what she wanted did he prevent himself from kissing away the worry in her eyes and the slight quiver of her lips.

He thought as he did so that never in his whole life, in all his many and often tempestuous love-affairs, had he ever felt as he did now.

No woman had ever affected him not only with a burning desire, but with a feeling that he recognised as reverence for her innocence and purity, and also with something else.

He could only describe it to himself as a spiritual awareness that he and Mariota belonged to each other and were meant to be joined as one since the beginning of time.

It was not only her beauty that held him spellbound, so that as he had said she haunted him both by day and by night, but there was also an aura of goodness that emanated from her and made him aware that she was not only exceedingly desirable, but also very, very precious as a person.

'I worship you,' he wanted to say to her.

But because they were so closely attuned he knew that she had to tell him what was on her mind before she could be sure of his love.

'You will be . . very shocked and perhaps also very . . angry,' Mariota began in a small voice, 'and I do not know how to . . tell you how desperately . . ashamed I am of . . what I have . . done.'

'What have you done, my precious?'

Mariota drew in her breath. Then in a voice that did not sound like her own she said:

'I . . I was with Jeremy when . . disguised as a Highwayman . . he . . held up your sister's coach and . . robbed her of her . . money!'

She could not look at the Earl as she went on, feeling as if every word had to be dragged from her lips, and to speak was an agonising pain:

'It was . . I who fired my pistol at . . you when I saw you pointing . . yours at Jeremy's back . . and which caused your horse to rear . . so that he . . threw you.'

She knew without looking at him that the Earl was staring at her incredulously. Then he asked:

'You were dressed as a man?'

'Y.yes . . Jeremy said it was safer . . and it would be dangerous for him if I did not . . go with him . . I could . . therefore not let him go . . alone.'

As Mariota spoke she thought that this was the end of everything that mattered, and that because he would be shocked and furious not only at her behaviour but at her perfidy in not telling him sooner, the Earl would walk away and leave her.

He would then go back to the house and somehow find a way of leaving immediately.

She would never see him again and her dreams of happiness would lie broken around her so that she might as well be dead.

Then suddenly, unexpectedly and astonishingly the Earl laughed.

As if she could not believe what she was hearing Mariota turned her face to look up at him and saw that his eyes were twinkling and he was laughing as if he could not help it.

Then he put out his hand and pulled her towards him.

'Oh, my darling, only you and your fantastic family could think of anything so unusual, so extraordinary, that I can hardly believe I am not taking part in some Restoration Comedy. I adore you!'

He put his arms around Mariota and held her so tightly that she could hardly breathe, let alone speak. Then he went on:

'How could I have imagined for one moment you would do anything so absurd and at the same time so dangerous? I promise you, my precious one, that it is something you will never do again.'

Mariota hid her face against his shoulder, and as he knew that she was crying, he said:

'You are not to cry, there is nothing to cry about.'

'I thought you would . . hate me . . and I would . . lose you.'

'You will never do that,' he answered tenderly. 'At the same time, I would find it humiliating that your first sight of me should have been when I fell off a horse, if it had not been a most effective if somewhat unusual introduction.'

His lips were against her forehead as he said:

'If that had not happened, I would have gone on to Madresfield and not even been aware that you existed. So all I can say is, my darling, thank God Jeremy needed some new clothes!'

Mariota looked up at him wonderingly, the tears on her cheeks and on her long eye-lashes.

'You . . realise that was . . why he wanted money?'

'I admit I have wondered once or twice,' the Earl replied, 'as you were so poor and according to Lynne existing on a diet of rabbit, how Jeremy could appear in the latest and most fashionable attire, made by what I know to be a very expensive Tailor.'

'You will not be . . angry with Jeremy?'

'Angry with him?' the Earl asked. 'I am so grateful to him for taking Elizabeth off my hands that I am just wondering what would be the best and most expensive wedding-present I could give them both.'

Mariota gave a little cry of joy.

'You understand . . you forgive us? How can you be so . . wonderful? How can there be such a kind and . . marvellous man in the world, and how could I have found . . him?'

The Earl did not answer. He merely kissed her and it was a long time later before Mariota asked:

'Y.you will not tell your . . sister about Jeremy?'

'No, of course not,' the Earl replied. 'It would be a great mistake, my darling, for your secret to be divulged to anybody except your husband, and I very much doubt if Jeremy will confide in his wife.'

'I did promise Jeremy that nobody will ever know,' Mariota said, 'but I had to tell . . you in case it created a . . secret between us which might have . . spoiled our love.'

'There will be no secrets between us,' the Earl said fiercely. 'I will take care of that! You are mine, Mariota, and I own every thought that comes into your head and every dream that you have when you are asleep.'

She gave a little laugh and he said:

'I have always in the past despised men who were jealous, but I shall be wildly jealous of you, and that is what happens when one is really in love.'

'You will never . . need to be jealous,' Mariota answered. 'For me you fill the whole world, the sky and the sea, and there is only you. It would be impossible for me when . . you are there to know that . . anybody else exists.'

The way she spoke, the depth of her voice and the little touch of passion that had never been there before was very moving.

The Earl kissed her again until she asked:

'What are we to say if we find your . . sister is waiting for you when we go . . back to the house? Surely she will think it . . strange that you did not go to Madresfield, as you intended, and she has doubtless come here to . . find you?'

'I have a feeling,' the Earl replied, 'that she will not be particularly agitated about us. She will be quite happy sitting talking to your father.'

'Papa loves having her to talk to.'

'And my sister *loves* being with him.'

The way he spoke made Mariota look at him in surprise.

'You . . do not mean . . ?' she began.

'Why not?' the Earl asked. 'Your father is a very hand-some man, and if my calculations are right he is only about forty-three. If you are not there to look after him, Mariota, as you will not be, then my sister could manage very efficiently.'

'I never thought of such a thing,' Mariota exclaimed. 'How stupid of me! But of course it is a wonderful idea, if only it comes true. Lady Coddington is so sweet and I know Papa has been very lonely, besides having been abjectly miserable since Mama died.'

She gave a little sigh before she added:

'We have all tried to do our best, but children are not the same as a . . wife.'

'Of course not,' the Earl agreed, 'and if you love our

135

children more than you love me, Mariota, I shall not only be very jealous, but also very unhappy.'

'I could never love . . anybody more than you,' Mariota answered. 'But . . it would be wonderful to have your children.'

She spoke impulsively, thinking that the Earl had sometimes seemed like a school-boy when he was ill, and it would be marvellous to hold his son in her arms, and know that he needed her and her love.

As if he understood what she was thinking the Earl said:

'How could I have ever imagined that I would be happy and my life complete without a family to fill my big house, and of course to ride my horses?'

Mariota laughed and he said:

'Do you realise, my darling one, I have never seen you on a horse? That is something else we will enjoy together, besides a million other things which will take me a lifetime to explain to you.'

He put his fingers under her chin and tipped her face up to his before he said:

'And now, without all the arguments I have had to endure, so far, I shall be able to give you all the things I want you to have: furs, jewels, in fact everything that makes a perfect background for your beauty.'

'It all sounds very . . exciting,' Mariota murmured, 'but the only thing I really want is . . your love.'

. . . .

The Countess of Buckenham kissed her father good-bye then kissed her new Step-mother with a warmth and affection that came from her heart.

Even now it was incredible that everything in her life had changed so dramatically, and yet so perfectly that it really seemed as if the Genie she had wanted to conjure up had waved his magic wand and granted all her wishes.

When she learned that Lady Coddington had promised to marry her father Mariota had not only realised the Earl's intuition was far more acute then hers, but it was also the best thing that could ever have happened.

'I thought it would be Jeremy who would do up Queen's Ford,' she said to the Earl, 'and make it as it was in the past. But that might have been embarrassing for Papa. Now I know that Noreen will enjoy every moment of supervising its restoration, just as Papa will.'

'Of course,' the Earl said, 'and I have already decided, although I have not yet had time to tell you about it, that I shall offer Jeremy and Elizabeth my house at Newmarket where they can live until they find a house of their own. I am sure that even before he buys anything as necessary as a bed, Jeremy will buy horses!'

'What a marvellous idea!' Mariota cried with delight. 'How kind and understanding of you!'

'I think when they return from their honeymoon,' the Earl went on, 'it would be a great mistake for them to have to stay with the Duke, so when you send your message to the *"Morning Post"* to let them know they can return, it would be a good idea to add that they should get in touch with you first. We can then explain to them exactly what has happened.'

Mariota slipped her hand into his.

'You think of everything!' she said. 'I cannot tell you what a relief it is not to know that I must do all the planning.'

'I have a feeling,' the Earl replied, 'that you will always be planning things for me, and when you have done so, pretending they were my ideas in the first place.'

Mariota laughed and put her cheek against his shoulder.

'How did you guess that that is the way I inveigle Papa into doing the things I want?'

'All women are born deceivers and schemers.'

Mariota looked at him quickly to see if he was condemning her then as she saw the smile on his lips and in his eyes she merely said:

'I love you . . and if I do get my own . . way it will only be through . . love.'

'That is what I am frightened of!' he answered, but she knew he was teasing her.

It was of course the Earl who planned their wedding

so perfectly that everybody agreed to his suggestions immediately.

Because Lady Coddington had no desire to return to her own house in London which she would have been obliged to do as soon as the Duke realised what had happened to his daughter, the Earl sent for his Chaplain in Oxfordshire to come to Queen's Ford.

Very early in the little Church in the Park he had married first Lord Fordcombe and Lady Coddington, then two hours later the Earl and Mariota.

It was Lord Fordcombe who said firmly that he had no wish to have even his daughters at his wedding.

'I am starting a new life,' he said, 'and a new chapter of my own history, and during the ceremony I want to think only of Noreen.'

Lynne had wanted to protest, but Mariota had understood.

Her father had loved her mother, and he had thought when she died that life would never be the same again.

He had therefore buried himself in his book and tried not even to think about what happened outside it.

Now in his new happiness he wanted, as he said himself, to start again and forget the suffering and misery of what had happened before.

He and Lady Coddington had therefore driven together from Queen's Ford to the Church in a closed carriage belonging to the Earl.

After they were married they came back to the house and were alone together without anybody disturbing them until two hours later when the new Lady Fordcombe drove back to the Church with Lynne, while Mariota followed in another carriage with her father.

Once again the Church was quiet and empty and there was no-one to stare at them and no friends to be surprised at the secrecy of the ceremony. But Mariota felt as if the Forde ancestors who meant so much to her father were all there, giving her their blessing.

She thought too when she and the Earl said their vows and were joined together there was music coming from the arched roof as if there was a choir of angels singing the melodies of her dreams.

Because the Earl, ever since they had first known they could be together, had heaped her with presents, she was wearing not only the most beautiful wedding-gown she could ever imagine, but also a wreath of diamonds on her head fashioned in the shape of flowers.

She had also a necklace and bracelet of the same stones which he told her were only the beginning of the gifts he wished to give her.

She knew when she looked in the mirror before she left the Church that she was not only beautiful, and exactly as if she had stepped out of her own dreams, but also the Earl's.

When he took her hand in front of the altar she felt so close to him in her mind, heart and soul, that she thought not even the Blessing of God could make them closer than they were already.

'We have belonged together all through Eternity,' Mariota thought and thanked God that they had found each other, and she was no longer alone and frightened, as she had been in the past.

'The only person who has been left out,' Lynne complained when she heard of all the plans that were being made by the Earl, 'is me! Jeremy is married, Mariota is to be married, and so is Papa. It is not fair!'

'I have not forgotten you,' the Earl replied. 'In fact Mariota and I have talked a great deal about you. Do you want to hear what we have decided?'

'I am glad you have even thought of me!' Lynne answered sarcastically.

'I have been to see Mrs. Fellows,' Mariota said, 'and she is delighted to have you to stay at the Grange with Elaine until the end of the summer. You will have your own horse to ride there, which you will keep in the Squire's stables, and there will be more horses in the winter so that you can hunt both from the Grange, if you wish to, or from here.'

'Hunt?' Lynne cried excitedly.

'But actually,' Mariota went on, 'you are going to do something very exciting first.'

'What is that?'

'Alvic thought it would be very educational, both for you and for Elaine,' Mariota replied, 'if you saw a little Europe in the Autumn, and improved both your French and Italian.'

Lynne's eyes were like stars.

'What do you mean?'

'Alvic has arranged,' Mariota went on, 'that you and Elaine with a Governess and a Courier and a number of other people to look after you, will go first to Paris where you will see the Museums, and will also be entertained by some friends of the Earl's who have girls of your age, and from there you will visit Florence and Rome.'

Lynne gave a cry that was a shriek of excitement.

'I cannot . . believe it! Can we . . really do that?'

'It is all arranged,' Mariota replied. 'Then next year you will "come out" and Papa will give a Ball for you here, and there will also be one in London, one at Buckenham House, and another in Oxfordshire.'

Lynne was speechless. Then she flung her arms around the Earl and kissed him.

'Only you could think of anything so wonderful!' she said. 'It is the most exciting thing I have ever heard!'

'I hoped you would think so,' the Earl replied, 'and I promise you that you will be the toast of St. James's! But I would also like you to be knowledgeable as well as beautiful.'

'I will be the cleverest débutante who ever made her curtsy to the King!' Lynne promised and the Earl laughed.

'How can you be so kind to my family and arrange anything so wonderful?' Mariota asked him when they were alone.

'I must confess it is an entirely selfish action on my part,' he replied, 'simply because I have no wish to see that worried look in your eyes or know that you are fussing over them when you should be fussing over me!'

She knew he was making light of what had involved a great deal of thought and planning, and she said:

'It is impossible to say "thank you" any more, so I

shall just say "I love you!" '

'That is all I want to hear,' the Earl said and kissed her.

Now as Lynne showered them with rose petals they ran down the steps to climb into the Phaeton which drawn by six horses was waiting for them, Mariota remembered her three wishes.

Already Queen's Ford seemed to glow with the glory which once again would be there when her father and his new wife had finished restoring it.

'Good luck! Have a lovely time!' Lynne was shouting and Mariota waved until the little party on the steps were out of sight.

Then as she moved a little closer to her husband, he looked down at her with an expression of happiness which made him appear younger and more handsome than he had ever looked before.

'Happy, my darling?' he asked.

'I am floating on clouds in a dream,' Mariota answered. 'Is it really true that we are married, and I am your wife?'

'I will answer that question a little later,' the Earl said, 'but I feel too as if I am driving across the sky rather than on the earth.'

They passed the little Church where they had been married, and Mariota said:

'I knew when you put your ring on my finger that the angels were singing, and I can still hear their music and feel that even your horses are moving to the rhythm of it.'

'You can play it to me when we get home,' the Earl said. 'It is something we have never had time to do until now.'

'I hope you will not be disappointed.'

'Could anything you do or say disappoint me?' the Earl asked. 'I love you so much, my darling, that I feel it would be impossible to love you any more, and yet I know that tonight when I hold you in my arms in my own house I will be aware of what I have always missed in the past, and our love will be even greater and more overwhelming than it is at the moment.'

'That is what I feel too,' Mariota said, 'and when I am really your wife . . all my dreams will have come true.'

141

She knew because she was so closely attuned to him that what she had said excited him.

Although he was too experienced a driver to hurry his horses unnecessarily she was aware that he was driving as fast as possible, so that they would reach his house in Oxfordshire without being over-tired.

Actually, because the Earl was so experienced with the reins, they turned in through the magnificent iron gates of Buckenham Park just before four o'clock and the sun, warm and golden, enveloped the great house with an aura of gold.

It was very different from Queen's Ford, and yet in its own way as beautiful and so large and magnificent that it was like its owner.

'Welcome home, my darling!' the Earl said gently.

Mariota looked at the house wide-eyed and felt because it was so very big and impressive a little afraid.

She put her hand on her husband's knee and said in a small voice:

'You will be . . there?'

'Always,' he answered, 'and because we are together, nothing else is of any importance.'

'Of course not,' Mariota agreed, and she was smiling.

There were a large number of servants waiting to greet them, and when they had drunk a glass of champagne with the Earl's secretary, Mariota had been taken upstairs to a bedroom where all the Countesses of Buckenham had slept since the house was built.

Like the State Rooms at Queen's Ford it was very impressive, but so large that she felt for the moment as if she might be lost beneath the painted ceiling supported by its marble and gold pillars, and the great draped bed surmounted by a coronet supported by cupids.

Then the Earl was beside her and when she had taken off her bonnet and her cloak he drew her into a *Boudoir* which adjoined her bedroom and communicated with his, and shut the door behind them.

The whole room was decorated with white lilies, camelias and orchids, but when she would have looked at them the

142

Earl swept her into his arms, and his lips were on hers.

He kissed her until she felt once again that he was lifting her even higher into the sky than she was already, the stars glittered around them, the sun burned in their breasts and the music that had been playing all day seemed to burst into a crescendo of glory.

'I love you!' the Earl said. 'I love you, darling, and now you are home, and we are together, I need never again be afraid of losing you.'

She knew as he spoke that he was still thinking of the suffering they had both endured when he had thought he must go to Madresfield and marry Elizabeth.

Mariota pressed herself closer to him and put her arm around his neck so that his face was near to hers.

'I love you . . I love you!' she said. 'And although your house is magnificent, I would feel just the same if we had to live in a cottage or even a cave in the mountains.'

Her voice was anxious as she went on:

'You have given me such . . marvellous presents . . but the most wonderful of them all are your kisses . . and I keep wondering how I can . . express my gratitude not only to you . . but also . . to God.'

'You can only thank me by loving me,' the Earl said. 'I want your love, and because it is mine, I am also grateful, very, very, grateful.'

He spoke almost as insistently as she had, then he gave a little laugh.

'And all this has happened,' he said, 'because Jeremy wanted some new clothes.'

Because it sounded so absurd, Mariota laughed too.

Then the Earl drew her across the Sitting-Room through a door at the end of it which led into his own bedroom.

It was even more magnificent than the one that was hers, and there was something too that was very masculine about it, which made it seem a very appropriate background for the Earl. 'You have had a long journey, my darling,' he said, 'but I also know that there are at least three hours to wait before dinner, and I think you should rest.'

'Yes . . of course,' Mariota said obediently. 'Shall I go to my own . . room?'

There was a little twist to the Earl's lips as he looked down at her which told her how happy he was.

'I want you to rest with me,' he said, 'and that is a polite word for it.'

As she suddenly realised what he meant her eyes dropped shyly and the colour rose in her cheeks.

'Oh, my darling,' the Earl said, 'I will not make you do anything you do not wish to do, but I have wanted for a very long time you to be my wife.'

Mariota looked at him questioningly and he explained:

'It may be only a few days by the calendar, but every minute I have not had you in my arms has seemed like a century, and every second at least a year, but whichever way you add it up, it has been far too long.'

Mariota gave a little laugh.

Then as the Earl pulled her closer and still closer to him she was conscious of the great curtain-draped bed behind them and the cupids that climbed up the carved posts and rioted over the golden canopy.

Everywhere she looked, Mariota thought, there was an emblem of love.

Then she could think of nothing except her husband, of his arms, his lips and the fire of love rising like burning flames within them both.

She had wished for love, and her wish had come true, and it was the arms of love which carried her into the great bed.

Their hearts beat to the music of love as the Earl kissed her, the stars fell down from the sky to cover them with love and angels carried them into a special Heaven where there was only real love which they would find together for all Eternity.